BETRAYED HONOR

IVANOV CRIME FAMILY, BOOK THREE

ZOE BLAKE

Poison Ink Publications

Copyright © 2021 by Zoe Blake

All rights reserved.

No part of this book may be reproduced in any form or by any electronic or mechanical means, including information storage and retrieval systems, without written permission from the author, except for the use of brief quotations in a book review.

Cover Design by Dark City Designs
Photographer: James Critchley

CONTENTS

Chapter 1	1
Chapter 2	9
Chapter 3	19
Chapter 4	29
Chapter 5	37
Chapter 6	42
Chapter 7	53
Chapter 8	64
Chapter 9	72
Chapter 10	79
Chapter 11	88
Chapter 12	97
Chapter 13	106
Chapter 14	116
Chapter 15	127
Chapter 16	132
Chapter 17	143
Chapter 18	151
Chapter 19	162
Chapter 20	175
Chapter 21	185
Chapter 22	191
Chapter 23	202
Chapter 24	211
Chapter 25	220
Chapter 26	231
Chapter 27	241
Chapter 28	247
Epilogue	254

About Zoe Blake   265
Also By Zoe Blake   267

NOTE FROM ZOE BLAKE

Here is the beautiful Russian song which helped inspire this book.

Dark is the Night
Composed by Nikita Bogoslovsky

Dark night, only bullets are whistling in the steppe,
Only the wind is wailing through the telephone wires, stars are faintly flickering ...
In the dark night, my love, I know you are not sleeping,
And, near a child's crib, you secretly wipe away a tear.
How I love the depths of your gentle eyes,
How I want to press my lips to them!
This dark night separates us, my love,
And the dark, troubled steppe has come to lie between us.
I have faith in you, in you, my sweetheart.
That faith has shielded me from bullets in this dark night ...
I am glad, I am calm in deadly battle:
I know you will meet me with love, no matter what happens.

Death is not terrible, we've met with it more than once in the steppe ...
And now here it looms over me once again,
You await my return, sitting sleepless near a cradle,
And so I know that nothing will happen to me!

Тёмная ночь

Темная ночь только пули свистят по степи
Только ветер гудит в проводах тускло звезды мерцают
В темную ночь ты любимая знаю не спишь
И у детской кроватки тайком ты слезу утираешь
Как я люблю глубину твоих ласковых глаз
Как я хочу к ним прижаться сейчас губами
Темная ночь разделяет любимая нас
И тревожная черная степь пролегла между нами
Верю в тебя в дорогую подругу мою
Эта вера от пули меня темной ночью хранила
Радостно мне я спокоен в смертельном бою
Знаю встретишь с любовью меня что б со мной ни случилось
Смерть не страшна с ней не раз мы встречались в степи
Вот и теперь надо мною она кружится
Ты меня ждешь и у детской кроватки не спишь
И поэтому знаю со мной ничего не случится

CHAPTER 1

*M*ikhail
Three years earlier.

"What the hell do you think you're doing?"

As the sharp edge of my voice cut through the chilly darkness of the bookshelf-lined study, Nadia turned, her bright blue eyes wide with shock. Her arm hung suspended in midair as the silver flask clutched in her hand stopped just before touching her lips.

The soft, bluish white glow from the moonlight streaming through the large windows illuminated her pale face. It gave her an ethereal quality, as if I had startled a beautiful specter during her nightly hauntings. The muted noises of dancing and laughter sounded a world away. Since we were in the far wing of the house, they might as well have been.

From this distance, no one would hear her cries for help.

Just over her shoulder, insolently lounging in her older brother's oxblood leather chair with his feet on the desk, was a man I didn't recognize, but not knowing his name would not prevent me from killing him.

He spread his arms wide, palms out. "Relax!" Foamy spittle fell onto his tie from his lips as he slurred the word. "She can have a swig or two. It's a party." He swung his head in Nadia's direction. The man took a moment to refocus his drunken gaze before giving her an exaggerated wink.

It was all I could do not to seize her in my arms and bodily carry her out of the room.

How dare she put herself in danger like this?

Wandering away from her own party to sneak a drink with some unknown man?

This wasn't like her.

Most of the guests were assholes in cheap suits and women in tight dresses reeking of even cheaper perfume. In other words, the usual crowd of business associates, political dignitaries and crime bosses that congregate at an Ivanov party. They were all here to celebrate Nadia's birthday. Well, truthfully, none of them were actually here to celebrate her birthday. Few could even pick her out of a lineup.

They were here for one reason, and one reason only: to get close to her brothers.

Each drawn to the unchallenged power the family wielded.

Each coming with a false smile and an open palm, hoping to curry favor and line their pockets.

Each ignoring the guest of honor, the birthday girl.

No wonder she had wandered off unnoticed, but only because I'd been occupied by dragging a drunk who had accosted her friend Yelena out the back.

The moment I returned, I knew she was gone. It had become a habit over the years to always look for her. As the Ivanovs' head of security, technically it was my job to watch over her, to protect her.

My job and my own private hell.

I wasn't sure which part angered me more.

That she had wandered off alone when the house was filled with strangers.

Or that she had wandered off with another man.

My fingers curled into a fist at my side.

If I can't have her, no one can.

It was an irrational and selfish thing to think, especially since I had never even so much as allowed myself to touch her, but then I wasn't thinking straight in that moment. Something tightened in my chest as I reined in a primal howl of *mine*.

As she fidgeted under my unrelenting gaze, her two front teeth sunk into the soft plump flesh of her lower lip. An adorable nervous tic of hers. My tongue flicked out over my lip as if I could taste the cherry sweetness of the flavored lip gloss I knew she liked.

Nadia bowed her head and turned. She leaned over, stretching her arm across the wide expanse of the polished oak desk, to hand the man his flask back. As she did so, the ruffled edge of her floral dress rode up the back of her thighs. She had the cutest freckle which peeked out from behind her hem, high on the back of her right thigh, just below the soft curve of her ass. I resisted the urge to tilt my head to the side in a juvenile attempt to catch a glimpse of her panties.

Christ.

Speaking of hell, that was precisely where I was going. Her two brothers would be the ones to send me there.

This was madness. If her brothers knew what I was thinking, they'd put a bullet in my head. My years of loyalty be damned.

The fact that Nadia had finally turned eighteen didn't matter. She may have been legal to touch, but that didn't make it less wrong. Nadia was the protected baby sister of the Ivanov family, and the very definition of forbidden fruit. I wouldn't blame Gregor and Damien for taking me to one of our off-grid warehouse locations and beating me bloody to within an inch of my life for even looking at her this way.

As she stood before me, she fidgeted with the charms on her silver bracelet and rambled, "Mikhail, this is Adam. Adam Fischer. He's Peter's older brother. You know Peter, right? Samara's boyfriend? Adam graduated several years ahead of us."

Fischer.

He wasn't Russian. Another strike against him. At least now I had a name for his tombstone.

Adam lifted his flask in a mock salute and called out, "Na zdorov'ye!" He then took a long gulp.

I cast an annoyed glance in Nadia's direction. She at least had the presence of mind to look embarrassed at Adam's incorrect use of a toast most Americans thought Russians used every time we took a sip of alcohol.

Adam leaned over to hand the flask back to Nadia. "Take another sip, sweet stuff."

Sweet stuff?

My control snapped. I surged forward.

Nadia sprang out of the way, a small cry of fear on her lips as she raised her arms.

I moved past her and swiped at Adam's feet, knocking them off the desk. My fists twisted into the extra fabric of his ill-fitting polyester suit blazer, and I wrenched him out of the chair. Even before knowing his name or hearing his voice, I'd known he wasn't Russian. A Russian man would never disgrace his hosts by wearing the same wrinkled suit he had worn into work that day to a celebrated event in someone's home.

I leaned in close to rasp in his ear. "YA vyrvu tebe glaznyye yabloki i zasunu ikh v tvoye degenerativnoye gorlo."

Adam's thin lips stretched wide over small teeth in a crooked smile as he shoved his forearms up, then against my wrists, breaking my grip. "Shove off so Natalia and I can get better acquainted. Don't worry," he sneered, "I'll hand her over to you once I'm done."

Since I had just told him I was going to rip out his eyeballs and shove them down his degenerate throat, that would not happen. After dragging him from behind the desk, I swung around and shoved him toward the door.

"Her name is Nadia, you piece of shit, and you'll touch her over my fucking dead body."

While we were matched in height, each over six feet tall, I had at least thirty pounds of muscle on him, which gave me an advantage. That, and the fact I was raised in the unforgiving icy wilderness of Siberia and not some cushy American suburb. Although I knew Adam didn't have any political power and wasn't connected to the Ivanovs' criminal enterprise, it still would look bad if I hauled him out of the party bloody and bruised. Against my better judgment, I would have to let him go with a warning to never go near Nadia again.

At least that was my plan until he took a swing at me. Then all bets were off.

Adam snatched a brass double-headed eagle figurine from the bookshelf nearby, and swung his arm wide, almost clipping me on the chin.

I took a step back and grinned. I slipped out of my suit jacket and tossed it onto the desk behind me. Slowly circling Adam as he continued to lurch about and swipe his arms at me, I rolled up my shirt sleeves.

Nadia's plea came from behind me. "Mikhail, don't. It's my fault."

I tossed her a look over my shoulder, and warned, "I will deal with you in a minute."

This time when Adam swung the brass figurine, it slipped out of his hand and sailed across the room. It almost hit Nadia in the shoulder before shattering the window behind her. With a snarl, I snapped my right arm out, hooking him under the chin with my fist. He staggered back. I hit him again and again. I didn't give a damn if he was drunk. If he was sober enough to toss a punch, he was sober enough to take one. The final time I swung out, I felt his cheekbone shatter beneath my knuckles. Adam fell to his knees, howling in pain as he clutched his face. A swift kick to the jaw silenced his cries.

As his body fell limply onto the Persian carpet, Ilya, one of my men, appeared in the doorway. "Alarm went off, signaling a breach."

Lowering onto my haunches, I wiped the blood from my knuckles onto Adam's shirt. Motioning with my head, I indicated the window. "Broken window." I rose and pointed to Adam. "Mr. Fischer has overstayed his welcome. Please see him out."

Ilya snatched Adam up under his arms and walked backwards as he dragged his limp body toward the door. "Consider it done, Boss."

As I followed him to the threshold, I instructed, "Ubedites', chto gosti nichego ne vidyat." The last thing I needed was a scene with the party guests.

Ilya nodded, then casually asked, "Should we kill him?"

There was a soft gasp behind me.

Ilya started as he looked past me, deeper into the dark room. "Izvini, Boss. YA yeye tam ne videl."

Of course he hadn't seen Nadia. It was a common occurrence. As the quiet little sister of the great Ivanov brothers, everyone often overlooked her.

Everyone but me.

At barely over five feet tall, Nadia didn't even come up to my shoulder. She was like a living doll. She had a light smattering of freckles over the bridge of her tiny nose, a delicate Cupid's bow of a mouth and an adorable bundle of soft strawberry blonde curls. Each time she nervously bit her lip, I wanted to do dark and dangerous things to her.

Yes, everyone else may look past her, but not me.

She was the first person I looked for when I entered a

room and the last one I thought of at night. Every time she left the house, even if it was only to go to school, I was on edge till she was back safely at home, under my control. The Ivanovs led a dangerous life with ruthless enemies who could strike at any moment. Nadia was a vulnerability, a weak point their enemies would think nothing of exploiting, but that would never happen. Not on my watch.

The number one rule in the Ivanov household was no one talked business in front of or within earshot of Nadia. It was the family's wish she never be aware of the extent of their criminal activities. As far as she was concerned, her father had owned a successful import and export business that he passed on to her brothers at his death. The intense security I and my staff provided were explained away as America being a dangerous country.

I waved off Ilya's apology. "Nichego, Ilya. Prosto delay, kak ya govoryu."

As soon as they were both gone, she spoke up, although her voice was barely above a nervous whisper. "I should rejoin the party. My mother will be looking for me."

With a flat palm, I pushed the door shut. I slid the heavy brass bolt that was secured just below the top of the door into place.

Turning, I faced Nadia. "You're not going anywhere."

CHAPTER 2

adia

Mikhail wasn't just angry. He was *pissed*.

I had snuffed out my spark of rebellion in coming to the study with Adam, leaving only a weak puff of smoke and the lingering smell of sulfur.

Smoke and sulfur, warning signs of the Devil's approach.

Judging by his thunderous expression and rage-filled eyes, Mikhail fit the bill perfectly.

Earlier tonight, I'd looked around the living room for the only two friends I had at *my* so-called birthday party. Yelena had been dancing with my brother Damien and looking very annoyed. She usually made it a point to keep her distance from him. My brother rubbed her the wrong way. She said it was because he's a Scorpio and she's a Sagittarius. Those two zodiac signs were not meant to get along. If Yelena believed in anything, it was the power of astrology.

Samara had been following her boyfriend Peter out of the living room toward the bedroom wing of the house. An unexpected stab of jealousy had caught me by surprise. I didn't begrudge Samara her boyfriend. Even though I didn't like him, I was still happy for her. I'd never been so lucky. Between my super scary overprotective brothers and my shyness, I'd never had a boyfriend.

There is also my stupid, pointless crush on Mikhail, my traitorous mind had whispered.

Just then, I'd caught the eye of someone staring at me from a few feet away. After capturing my gaze, he sauntered toward me. He was Peter's older brother, Adam. He'd graduated a few years ahead of us.

Reaching into his blazer, he pulled out a small silver flask. "Want some?"

Glancing around, I could no longer see Damien or my mother. Gregor, I knew, was outside on the patio having a cigar. I refused to acknowledge I looked for Mikhail as well, although I didn't see him either.

I mean, why not? I was eighteen now. I was tired of always being the good girl everyone could rely on to sit quietly in a corner and obey all their rules without question. "Sure."

I turned my back on the guests to face the wall. Gripping the cold metal flask, I tipped the contents into my mouth. I smashed my lips together and tried to contain the cough forcing its way out of my lungs. I was unsuccessful.

A hard slap on my back from Adam forced a second harsh cough. "Easy, sweet stuff."

I gave him a weak smile as I wiped a small drop of liquid off my chin with the back of my hand.

He twisted his shoulders and also took a long draft from the flask. He winked and said, "That's good whiskey."

Whiskey. So that's what was currently burning my insides like molten metal on water. My experience with alcohol was limited to lukewarm beer passed around behind the stands after a football game at school and the occasional sip of champagne at a family party.

I nodded and rasped past the pain in my throat, "Yep, good whiskey."

He motioned with his head. "This party is lame. Let's find someplace quiet and have some fun."

I hesitated. Neither my brothers nor Mikhail would like me wandering off alone with someone, even if it was a guest from my party. Gregor had lectured me before the event began that, as usual, there would be business associates of the family here and I should behave accordingly. My family often entertained for business reasons. My birthday was just an excuse. The rules for when they entertained had been drummed into me since I could walk.

No talking to anyone unless they introduced me to them.

No listening in on conversations that were none of my concern.

No leaving the primary event space alone or with

anyone, not even to my bedroom, without telling my brothers or a security staff member.

Never answer any questions from anyone, no matter how innocent they may sound.

To say my family was overprotective was an understatement. Something about their import-export business had always meant security guards with guns patrolling around the house. Since they had been a fixture in my life since I was a little girl, I just got used to them. Although I think the reason had more to do with my family's ancestry. Once a Russian, always a Russian, no matter if I was actually born in America. A Russian never quite lost their distrust of those around them, or the government. It was ingrained deep within our DNA.

Adam grabbed my hand as he put his other hand over his heart. "Come on, sweet stuff. Don't break my heart. Let's go."

Allowing myself to be pulled away, I cast a quick glance over my shoulder but didn't see anyone observing us.

I should have known better.

Even when he wasn't in the room, Mikhail was always watching.

He was so intense and brooding. I couldn't help but think, or perhaps it was just wishful hoping, that we had a connection, that we were kindred spirits.

I, too, stayed to the outer edges of those around me, quietly watching but rarely speaking. Except with Mikhail, it was a dedication to his job as our protector that kept him in the role of silent observer. For me, it was shyness and being the invisible little sister of the Ivanov brothers.

I had none of the arrogance or swagger of my brothers. Everything came so easily for them. They walked into a room and commanded the attention of everyone in it just by the power of their presence. It wasn't the same for me. Half the time people forgot I was even there. I wasn't really known for being *me*. I was Gregor and Damien's baby sister; that was my entire identity.

There was something dangerously comforting about allowing someone else to define you. I didn't really have to be my own person. There was no pressure to distinguish myself as intelligent or talented or skilled in something useful. What would be the point? No matter what I did, I would always be defined foremost as the baby sister of the Ivanov brothers.

Mikhail had been my one and only crush since he first started working for my brothers two years ago. All the boys at school were silly and immature compared to Mikhail. None could come close to his intense presence. He was the quintessential strong and silent type, like Edward from *Twilight* without the weird sparkly vampire vibe.

So, like a silly schoolgirl, I had admired him from afar, knowing it would never come to anything. For starters, he was close to five years older than me. He probably only dated sophisticated women. Women who were old enough to drink and had their own apartments. I was a nobody to him, just part of his work, a warm body they expected him to protect.

Except now, for the first time, that overwhelming,

super intense gaze was directed entirely at me. After getting used to being overlooked as the Ivanovs *invisible* baby sister, I suddenly felt so very much *seen*. It made me feel exposed and vulnerable. What if he guessed I had a crush on him? I would literally die. I needed to get out of this room and away from him.

I took a few steps back till the sharp edge of the desk pressed against my thighs. I licked my dry lips and tried to swallow past the choking fear that was threatening to close my throat. "I know I broke the rule about wandering off."

His dark eyes turned cold and hard. His words seethed through clenched teeth, causing a small tic to twitch high on his right cheek. "You're goddamn right you broke the rule about wandering off."

I started. Mikhail had never cursed at me before. In fact, he had never even raised his voice to me. Usually he barely spoke to me, and even then, it was only the simplest of polite niceties, *good morning* and *good evening*, that sort of thing. If I didn't occasionally catch his blue gaze watching me, I'd have guessed he didn't know I was alive.

Resisting the urge to stamp my foot, I crossed my arms over my chest and fired back defensively, "There's no need to yell at me."

Mikhail stormed toward me.

With a cry, I scurried around the desk, tripping over the thick rubber roles of my Doc Martens as they caught on the plush fibers of the black and royal blue Persian carpet beneath my feet. Despite there now being a large, solid oak desk between us, I still didn't feel safe. It was hard processing that thought.

I'd never felt unsafe around Mikhail before, quite the opposite in fact, but something had changed. I couldn't explain it. It was as if someone had flipped a switch. The air crackled with tension. My pulse raced, and my hands shook as adrenaline pumped through my veins, as if my body also sensed the change in the room's atmosphere, the shift in our dynamic, the danger.

Part of the problem was he was just so *big*. Everything about him was outsized, from his imposing height to the thick muscles in his arms. He was like a warm-blooded statue of a Roman god. On top of him towering over my much smaller frame, he also had the authority advantage that automatically came with being older.

Inhaling deeply through his nose, he cupped his right fist with his left palm and slowly and methodically cracked his knuckles. His handsome face was all hard lines and edges, from his razor-sharp cheekbones to his narrowed eyes.

The tense silence in the room stretched.

All that I could hear was the unrelenting tick, tick, tick of a brass clock tucked between some old leather volumes on a shelf behind me.

Tick tick tick.

It matched the rapid beating of my heart.

Tick tick tick.

Or the ticking of a time bomb.

Tick tick tick.

Turning my head slightly, my gaze shot to the locked door several feet away. The heavy metal bolt was out of my reach. Why couldn't I be tall like my brothers? Still, maybe if I banged on the door someone would hear me.

Mikhail's eyes followed my gaze. "You'll never make it."

"You can't just keep me prisoner in here."

"Watch me."

"This is insane. The guests will notice I'm gone."

"No, they won't."

The cruel truth of his words pierced my heart. He was right. Both Gregor and Damien seemed preoccupied with their own problems tonight. My mother was too busy playing hostess. Samara was with her boyfriend, and Yelena was probably still dancing. I had already been gone over a half an hour, and no one had come looking for me.

No one except Mikhail.

Mikhail circled toward me. Alarmed, I moved as well, trying to keep the desk between us. Our cat-and-mouse game ended with him standing between me and the door. My boots crunched on the broken glass from the window as an icy breeze against my bare legs sent a chill up my back. I could just catch the dark earthy scent of tobacco smoke drifting into the room from outside.

It must have been from Gregor's cigar. I could yell for help through the opening in the jagged glass, but then Gregor would know I had broken his rule about wandering off during a party, and that I had let someone into his private study who then broke his window. Oh, and *bonus,* that I had been drinking. Even though it was just a sip of whiskey, I'd be grounded till I was twenty-one, if not longer.

I lowered my head. My only option was to try to

reason with Mikhail. "I know you're mad at me for drinking when I'm only eighteen but– "

Mikhail placed his hands on the polished surface of the desk and leaned in. Over the last two years, I had only ever seen him in a suit or dressed head to toe all in black with a black long-sleeved thermal shirt and black cargo pants. This was the first time I was seeing him without a suit jacket and with his dress shirt sleeves rolled up. His arms were covered in brightly colored tattoos.

They were in the traditional Russian Khokhloma style, which made sense. One of the few things I knew about Mikhail was that he was an orphan from Siberia. Khokhloma was a very distinctive folk art style from that area of Russia. On his right forearm in brilliant oranges, reds, and blacks was a large bear standing on its hind legs surrounded by intricate swirls and various flowers. On his left was a rising Phoenix in the same bold color scheme.

It looked scary and sexy as hell at the same time. They made the little heart tattoo I had gotten on a whim on my hip last summer with Yelena and Samara seem like a silly tiny pink smudge.

The corner of his upper lip rose in a snarl. "I'm way beyond mad, kroshka."

Kroshka?

I had to have heard him wrong. There was absolutely no way the stoic-barely-knows-I'm-alive Mikhail Volkov just called me his *little poppet*, a common endearment for a man's girlfriend in Russia. I didn't think I'd ever been alone with him for this long, and it was obviously messing with my head. While no one was missing me now, eventually they would bring out the birthday cake and notice I was gone.

I had to get out of this room. Especially before I blurted out something stupid like *I think you're hot*.

Hopefully, it wouldn't come to that. Hopefully, I would leave this room and Mikhail would go back to not knowing I was alive and forget all about this. I'd just have to come up with some excuse for the window. That was easy enough.

"I promise I'll tell my mom and Gregor all about this — after the party. I'll take my punishment later."

He stood up to his full height. "Oh, I think you'll take your punishment now."

My eyes widened. How dare he think he could punish me as if I were nothing more than a misbehaving child? In a rash move, I stepped out from behind the safety of the desk to confront him. "You're not one of my brothers, or my boyfriend. You don't have any authority over me."

"The hell I don't," he ground out.

"Poshel na khuy, Mikhail!"

I knew I was in trouble the moment I said it.

CHAPTER 3

M*ikhail*

Fuck you? There was no way I'd heard her correctly.

The last thing I needed in this moment was a reminder I wasn't her boyfriend and had no authority over her.

Never mind the almost five-year difference in our ages. I could never be more than her brothers' employee to her. This wasn't about money. I had plenty of that. Her brothers paid well and often cut me in on some of their more lucrative deals. I had tens of millions of dollars stashed away in banks around the world.

This was something way more important than money. It was about family, about having a name, a reputation, a history. I had none of that. I was an unwanted bastard left on the cold cement steps of an orphanage deep in Siberia. A nobody, and there was no way they would allow Nadia

Ekaterina of the powerful Ivanov mafia family to date, let alone marry, a nobody.

But that didn't mean I was okay with my sweet innocent Nadia saying *fuck you* to me.

My eyes narrowed. I exhaled a harsh breath then ground out, "What the hell did you just say to me?"

Her cheeks flushed a deep red. She avoided my gaze and whispered, "You heard me."

I lunged.

A short scream burst from her lips as she turned to run, but she never stood a chance.

I snaked an arm around her waist and yanked her against me, pulling her close, the front of her body flush against mine. The thin fabric of her floral babydoll dress was fisted in my hand at her lower back, forcing the already short hem up even further. With my other hand, I reached around and palmed her ass. I jerked her hips forward, letting her feel the hard ridge of my cock.

As I leaned my head down, my lips almost brushing hers, I asked, "Was that an invitation?"

I watched as her gaze shifted to my mouth. She had the most beautiful light blue, almond-shaped eyes. They were the color of the sky after a snowstorm, blue with just hints of grey.

She licked her lips. "Mikhail, I—"

I claimed her mouth. She tasted like cherry lip gloss and whiskey. My tongue swooped in, giving hers no quarter. She hesitantly flicked the tip of her tongue against mine. The innocence of her response was almost my undoing. Groaning, I pressed further. Grinding my mouth against hers till I tasted the copper tang of blood. It only spurred me on.

Two years of pent-up desire snarled to life and snapped its leash. I was a man possessed. Too long, I had been a shadow in her life, always clinging to the edges, but never allowing myself the light of her gaze or smile. Forcing myself to survive on the slightest accidental brush of her hand or the sound of her laughter or the scent of her perfume as she passed. Knowing it was wrong to even think of her, dream of her. She was too naïve, too good, for the touch of my unclean hands. I knew I would only corrupt her. I never counted on a primal rage overtaking all rational thought at the idea of another man touching her. I guess I vainly hoped she would always remain sweet and innocent, sheltered in the secure fortress I had built around her.

Tonight, she'd broken her family's rules for the first time. I glimpsed a future of her as an adult, free to do as she pleased, no longer under my protection, and every fiber of my being howled in protest.

I was risking the fires of hell but didn't give a damn. If she was fated to lose her innocence, to be tainted by the evils of the world around her, then I would be the demon to do it.

She was mine, and that was final.

Surging forward, I slammed her against the bookshelf. The impact caused several figurines and a few books to crash to the floor. I moved my hand from her ass to caress the soft skin of her thigh before cupping her left leg under the knee and lifting it high to cradle my side. I shifted my stance and ground my hips against her core. Her softness barely eased the hard pulsing ache as my cock lengthened.

With my free hand, I palmed her right breast through her dress, but it was not enough. With a growl, I tore at the neckline, rending the fabric down the front till it slipped off her shoulder. Her skin was so pale, it was luminous. She wore only a simple, pastel yellow cotton bra, the sight of which nearly drove me mad, more so than the most expensive piece of lace lingerie from Paris could have done. Slipping my fingers beneath the strap, I wrenched it down. The movement left faint ruddy scratch marks on the curve of her shoulder and the top of her breast. I leaned down and latched onto one perfect rosy nipple like a man starved. I scraped the delicate flesh with my teeth as I pulled her deeper into my mouth. Unable to resist, I bit down, not hard, but hard enough.

Nadia cried out and tried to pull away. "Mikhail, wait—"

I was too lost in a fog of lust and rage to hear her cries.

I fisted the fabric of her dress and pulled it off her right shoulder. Clawing at her bra, I ripped it down. I didn't relent till I exposed both of her beautiful breasts. I cradled them both in my palms. It was shocking to see the difference between her creamy unflawed skin and my tanned and fight-scarred hands, the very embodiment of pure innocence versus impure sinfulness.

I pushed my face between her breasts and inhaled the sweet, delicate scent of her perfume, knowing the scruff of my five o'clock shadow would scrape her skin. The tip of my tongue flicked out to lick her skin. I needed to know if she tasted as sweet as I imagined she would. I pulled her other nipple into my mouth and ruthlessly teased it with the sharp edge of my teeth.

Her fingernails dug into my shoulders as she pleaded, "Please, Mikhail, not so hard."

Moving both my hands to her small waist, I kicked her legs open wider till she was unbalanced. Her only recourse was to cling to my arms. I then licked the smooth column of her neck. I could taste the rapid beat of her heart on my tongue. With the tip, I traced the delicate shell of her ear. I lifted the hem of what was left of her dress. The back of my knuckles caressed the warm cotton of her panties.

I traced the seam of her pussy through the fabric with the tip of my finger. "Are you wet for me, kroshka?"

Her head shifted from side to side. Her eyes were squeezed shut. "Please, I don't… I can't…." she whispered, her voice trailing off on a breathy moan.

I slipped my hand inside her panties, palming her. My middle finger pushed between her nether lips, seeking her wet heat. Thrusting inside, I reveled in the way her body tightened around me. My head fell back as a surge of almost painful desire spiked down my spine straight to my shaft. I thought of that same tight hole clenching around my cock. I thrust a second finger in.

Nadia rose on her toes as her pretty pink mouth opened on a gasp. "Ow! It's… it's…."

My lips kissed the corner of her mouth. "Shhh, baby. Be a good girl and open for me."

I kissed her again, matching the thrust of my tongue with the thrust of my fingers. She was slick and ready for me, but still too tight to take all nine inches of my thick shaft.

I forced a third finger inside of her.

Nadia broke our kiss and cried out. Her small hand reached down to wrap ineffectually around my wrist as she whimpered, "Stop, it hurts."

With my free hand, I broke her grasp. Interlacing my fingers with hers, I lifted her arm high over her head and pinned it against the leather bindings of the books behind her. Her silver charm bracelet jingled and chimed with the movement.

I rasped against her neck, "That's it, baby. Take it. Take the pain."

The pad of my thumb swirled over her clit, applying just enough pressure to make her hips squirm, as I continued to thrust my three fingers into her tight pussy, opening her, preparing her. My abdomen muscles clenched as the pressure increased along my shaft. "Baby, I can't wait any longer. Mne nuzhno tebya trakhnut'." Christ, it was true. I needed to fuck her like I needed my next breath.

Turning, I swiped an arm across half of Gregor's desk, sending several ledgers, pens, and a small lamp crashing to the ground.

I bent her over the desk. Pushing my hand into her soft strawberry blonde curls to hold her down, I flipped the hem of her dress up, exposing her cotton panties. With a swift twist of my hand, I tore them off her body.

Nadia flattened her palms on the desk and pushed up her torso with a shocked cry, but the pressure from my hand forced her prone again. Circling my palm over her ass and hip, I growled, "Were you a bad girl, tonight?"

Something sick and twisted rose up in me. I wanted to voice all the dirty things I wanted to do to her. I wanted to see that angel cheek of hers blush in horror and fascination at the crude sexuality of my words. I wanted her to feel the pain of desire and the release of pleasure. I wanted it all. Every piece of her. Every gasp. Every breath. Every inch of her skin. Every clench of her body. It all now belonged to me.

She tried to look at me over her shoulder, but my grip on her hair prevented it. "What?"

Raising my arm, I brought the flat of my hand down on her ass. The crack of skin against skin reverberated around the room. A bright crimson handprint marred her perfect skin. "Were you a bad girl?"

Nadia cried out, "Oh my God!"

I spanked her again. "Answer me."

She sniffed. "Please, don't spank me. It hurts."

Ignoring her pleas, I spanked her twice, once on each cheek. She bounced up on her toes as much as her clunky Doc Martens would allow. "Ow!"

I pushed my hand between her legs and teased her clit with the tip of my finger. "I want an answer, kroshka."

"Yes! Yes! I was bad."

I slipped a finger just inside and swirled it, wanting to tease the sensitive nerves right at her tight entrance.

I pulled her hair, just enough to give her a sharp sting. "I want to hear you say you were a bad girl. Let me hear those dirty words from that sweet mouth of yours."

Slipping the edge of my hand between her now warm

ass cheeks, I teased her tiny, puckered hole with the pad of my thumb. My cock strained against the fastening of my trousers at the thought of one day taking her there, deep and hard, till she cried for mercy.

Her bottom clenched as she tried to shimmy her hips away from my invasive touch. "Oh my God! Not... not there!"

"Say it. Say what I want to hear, and I'll stop," I commanded.

"I was a bad girl," she whimpered. Her breath fogged the polished surface of the desk.

I pushed her dress up higher, bunching it at her lower back. It was then I saw it: a tiny pink heart tattoo, high up on her left hip.

"Is this a fucking tattoo?" I growled.

Images of her exposing her body in some seedy tattoo parlor to be pawed by some degenerate convict as he pierced her flesh with his needle over and over again flashed across my mind. Now was not the time, but heads were going to roll when I found out who was guarding her the day she slipped away to get this done.

Her voice was high-pitched and tense as she squeaked, "Yes."

I leaned over her prone body and nipped at her ear. "Looks like you just gave me another reason to punish this cute little ass of yours."

Her only response was a low, throaty moan.

With my knee between her legs, I pushed at her inner thighs, opening her. I lowered the zipper on my pants and pulled my cock free. Wrapping my fingers around the thick shaft, I pumped my fist up and down a few times to ease the mounting pressure. I threw my head back and closed my eyes, trying to rein in the overwhelming desire to pound ruthlessly into her pliant body, knowing if I thrust into her sweet pussy at this moment, I might tear her in two.

I took a deep steadying breath through clenched teeth and opened my eyes to find Nadia staring at me from over her shoulder. Her bright blue eyes were wide with unshed tears as her lower lip trembled. I followed her gaze to my fist.

She was staring at my large cock like some frightened virgin.

Jesus Christ.

A virgin.

I was a monster.

In the heat of my rage and desire, I had forgotten Nadia was a virgin.

The very innocence that drew me to her was the very thing I had deliberately thrust out of my mind the moment my hands touched her. I had treated her no better than a shluha vokzal'naja, a train station whore. Rudely thrusting her untutored body into my world of dark and twisted desires that involved supplication and pain as a means to achieve higher depths of pleasure. My filthy touch had tainted her gentle innocence.

It would only take a deeper thrust of my fingers to confirm my suspicions, but it wasn't necessary. I knew deep in my bones she was untouched. She was too sheltered not to be. Between her family's name and the fierce reputation of her brothers, Nadia had never even been on a date, let alone had a boyfriend.

Even if someone had managed to get past our security for long enough to get that close to her, there was no doubt in my mind I would have known about it. Mainly because her brothers would trust me with the disposal of the body of whoever had dared to touch their little sister.

The same little sister who was at this moment half naked and bent over a desk, ready for me to fuck her from behind.

Trakhni menya, I'm a dead man.

CHAPTER 4

Nadia

MIKHAIL STEPPED AWAY FROM ME, his gaze filled with horror.

He turned his back to me, and I heard the ragged metal clicks of him zipping up his pants.

I shoved the hem of my dress down as I straightened, wincing at the slight warm sting that still radiated across my ass from his erotic spanking. I pulled up my bra straps and clutched at the remnants of my dress while watching his agitated pacing, afraid to speak.

Oppressively silent tension once more filled the room.

The ticking time bomb had returned.

Tick, tick, tick.

Mikhail ran a hand through his hair as he paced a few steps away from me.

Tick, tick, tick.

I sunk my teeth into my lower lip. Catching my reflection in the window to my right, I quickly smoothed down my hair, which had become a riot of wayward curls. The reflection that stared back at me was nothing more than a watery pale ghost with unnaturally enormous, anxious eyes. Although there was no hint of color in my mirrored image, I could feel the heat on my crimson-blushed cheeks.

As I stared down at my boots, I broke the silence. "I'm sorry. I don't know what I did wrong."

Mikhail turned and stormed toward me, stopping barely a breath away. He raised both arms as if to reach for me but then paused. His fingers curled into fists, and he clenched his jaw. "Don't. Don't do that."

I took a step toward him, already missing his warmth. "Do what? Mikhail, I don't understand what just happened."

Without responding, he turned, and once again paced.

Tick, tick, tick.

Not knowing what else to do, I bent to retrieve the lamp from the floor and set it back on the desk. I then kneeled to gather up the ledger books and the loose papers that had fallen free from them. My brothers followed my father's same quirky habit of preferring physical ledger books to a computer or accounting software. I once offered to help teach my father QuickBooks. I thought it might be a way for us to bond if I showed an interest in the family business. He just yelled nonsensical things about the government being able to trace those transactions and them being discoverable in court and ordered me out of his office, all the while muttering about the uselessness of daughters.

I guess it was fitting Mikhail was rejecting me in the very same room my own father had years ago.

Tears ran down my cheeks. Feeling silly and foolish, I swiped them away with the back of my hand but more continued to flow. Just then, gigantic hands fell on my shoulders. I looked up to see Mikhail down on his haunches before me. He had moved so silently, I started at his sudden nearness.

With his steady grasp, he drew me to my feet. I had to tilt my head back to look into his eyes. He was so very tall. The top of my head barely reached his shoulder. I had always liked that about him. I had spent countless nights wondering what it would feel like to just walk up and press my cheek to his chest as his muscular arms wrapped around me.

He cupped my face. His hands felt slightly calloused compared to the smoothness of my own. His thumbs swept over my cheeks, wiping the tears away. There was such a sadness to his gaze. His eyes were the brightest sapphire blue I had ever seen, so unlike my unremarkable bluish grey ones. It made his gaze that much more intense and mesmerizing. I held my breath, dreading what he may be about to say.

"My sweet kroshka. My little poppet. It is I who am sorry. What I have done is unforgivable."

Reaching up, I wrapped my hands around his wrists. "Don't say that. I wanted it. I still want it. I want you!"

His gaze dropped to my chest, and he softly swore. The ripped neckline of my dress had sagged off of one shoulder, exposing the top of my breast. There was the faint outline of a bite mark and several bright red scrape marks from the bristle on his jaw.

His fingertips lightly traced the marks. "They should shoot me like a rabid dog for doing this to you. You are far too pure to be subjected to the brutal touch of someone like me."

I could feel my chance at finally being with Mikhail slipping through my fingers. "No. I told you. I wanted it."

"You are too young to know what you want."

"I'm eighteen now!"

Mikhail dropped his hands and stepped back. "Exactly. Christ, you're practically still a child, and I was treating you like... like a... *fuck*." He rubbed his eyes with his hand.

I swiped at the fresh tears falling down my cheeks. "I thought this meant you liked me."

He wrapped his hand around the back of my head and pulled me close. I placed my hands on his chest. I could feel the steady beat of his heart and desperately wanted to press my cheek to it like in my dreams. The spicy, masculine scent of his aftershave tickled my nose. I couldn't help but smile. There was just something so *girlfriend-boyfriendy* about being so close to a man I could smell the faint remnants of his aftershave from earlier that morning.

His head dipped to the side as he stared at my mouth. Self-conscious, I licked my lips and felt the low vibrations of a growl emanating from deep inside his chest with my fingertips. "Babygirl, *like* is far too tame of a word for what I feel for you."

Elated, I rose on my toes and lifted my arms to wrap

my hands around his neck, wanting more than anything to once again feel his mouth on my own. I had only been given the tiniest taste of what his kisses felt like and already craved more. It was everything I imagined it would be. The feel of his lips was like when a rollercoaster paused at the very top of a sharp incline. In that moment, I was both terrified and thrilled. My body would brace for the impact of the g-forces while my brain tried to reconcile the excitement I felt from putting myself in such mortal danger.

He broke our embrace and took a deliberate step back. "This can never happen again, Nadia. You need to understand that. You are an Ivanov. You are meant for better."

"Don't say that. I don't want better. I want you. I lov—"

"Stop," he roared. "Don't say another word."

Tick, tick, tick.

"Is this about my brothers? I can talk to them."

"Do you honestly think I would let anyone, even your brothers, stand in the way of something I wanted? No, baby, this isn't about your brothers, but this is about honor. Your family's honor, and my tattered sense of honor. This is about me being far too old and far too tainted for someone as innocent and guileless as you."

"That's not true!"

He snatched at the neckline of my dress. "Goddamn it, Nadia. Look at your dress. I did this to you. I tore at it, and you, like a fucking animal. Christ, I would have taken you like one as well if we hadn't stopped."

I wrapped my arms across my chest and squeezed them tight, trying to contain the tremors that were racking my body with each fatalistic word he uttered.

With another muttered curse, Mikhail grabbed his discarded suit jacket and wrapped it over my shoulders.

He placed a finger under my chin to force my tearful gaze to his own. "This ends here and now. I would only bring you pain, kroshka."

"Don't I have a say in this?"

"No, my decision is final. As far as I'm concerned, this never happened."

"I could tell my brothers." It was a petulant thing to say, and I regretted it the moment I said it.

He nodded sagely. "You could."

We both knew I wouldn't. I wasn't as naïve as my family assumed. I knew some things they did weren't exactly legal. It was hard not to notice that my brothers were both feared and respected by the influential people who often came to our house. I was sure they wouldn't hurt Mikhail, but they would definitely fire him, and maybe even get him deported back to Russia, which meant I might never see him again.

I didn't trust myself to speak. Mikhail wrapped his arm around my shoulders and gently guided me to the door. I swiveled my head to survey the destruction we had left behind. "What about the mess?"

"I'll take care of it. First, let me take care of you."

Fresh tears welled up in my eyes. His voice was back to the distant, professional tone he always used with me. Gone was the gravelly voice full of passion and need.

Mikhail escorted me to my bedroom and waited outside my door for me to change. When I emerged, he surveyed me from head to toe and gave an approving smile. We walked down the long dark hallway without speaking. At the end, I could see flashes of warm light and hear the laughter and music from the guests. It felt like we were travelers returning from a distant planet back to civilization.

Could it really have been only an hour that had passed? It felt like a lifetime. In the span of a few brief minutes, I had glimpsed a future with Mikhail and then lost it. Having it ruthlessly wrenched from my grasp, not because of who I was, but because of who my family was. It wasn't fair.

We stopped just out of sight of the guests.

I tried to plead with him one more time. "Please, Mikhail, can we at least talk about this?"

He refused to even look at me. "No, this was a mistake. One we'd both be better off forgetting. We'll never speak of this again. You need to get back to your big party before you're missed."

I pressed my hand to the center of my chest. A *mistake*. In his eyes, I was nothing more than a mistake. The word had caused a physical stab of pain. I looked down, genuinely surprised not to see blood.

Mikhail shifted. He placed a warm hand on the side of my face and leaned down to place a chaste kiss on my forehead. "S Dnem rozhden'ya."

Happy birthday? The last thing I was having was a happy birthday.

I closed my eyes and leaned into his touch as I held my breath.

Please.

Please say it.

Just say it.

Please.

It would've given me at least a tiny shred of hope.

Mikhail paused.

I waited.

With a resigned sigh, he turned and walked back down the dark hallway, each step taking him further away from me.

Kroshka. I had so desperately wanted him to say the endearment. I wanted to be his little poppet at least one more time. I was so elated when he called me it earlier. If I had known that would be the last time, I would have savored it. I would have clasped it to my heart and played it repeatedly in my mind.

I turned to watch him go, willing him to turn around, begging him silently in my mind to at least glance back.

He didn't.

Tick, tick, boom.

CHAPTER 5

Mikhail

I RETURNED to the party in time to see the cake with its eighteen lit candles being brought in. The guests launched into a drunken rendition of Gena the Crocodile's song, our version of *Happy Birthday*.

My poor babygirl looked anything but happy.

The soft glow of the candles gave her pretty blue-grey eyes a stormy sadness.

Fuck. I needed to stop this. Thinking like this would get me killed, or worse. And yes, there were worse things than death. Several occasions throughout my time with the Ivanov brothers, I'd personally been the fate worse than death for many a man.

She wasn't mine.

Never would or could be.

It would not only be betraying her brothers, but her as

well. I would be taking advantage of what was probably only a schoolgirl's crush.

I flexed my hand before balling it into a fist. I could still feel the warmth of her skin against my palm. I couldn't believe I had taken things so far. Not only had I lost control with her, but I had also shown her a side of myself I'd never intended for her to see. The animalistic side that wanted nothing more than to toss her over my shoulder, drag her back to my cave, and fuck her senseless for days. The side that wanted her on her knees, begging with her eyes for me to allow her to breathe as my cock was shoved deep down her throat. The dark and twisted side that wanted her crying for mercy as I ruthlessly pounded into her tight asshole. My sexual preferences were too dark, too perverse, for an innocent such as she, and that would be true even if there wasn't my loyalty to her brothers or our age difference to consider.

I owed everything to her brothers. In a world where only family or connections going back generations were trusted, they took a chance on an arrogant army sergeant with nothing but a cheap bottle of Moskovskaya vodka and half a pack of counterfeit cigarettes to his name.

I shook my head.

My name.

What name?

Mikhail Volkov?

It *was* nothing. It *meant* nothing.

Mikhail Volkov. That was it. No middle name to hint at my heritage, because I had none.

Volkov?

That wasn't even a proper surname.

It was the name of the orphanage in a tiny coal-mining town named Cheremkhovo in Siberia, where my mother abandoned me within hours of my birth, with the umbilical cord still hanging limp and cold from my stomach as if it had never been connected or even received the warmth or lifeblood from her body.

In Cheremkhovo, I had two choices: black powder or lead.

I would either die from black lung after a desolate life underground in the mines, or I could become a soldier and risk death by a bullet. Either way, all roads led to a messy end to a useless life.

At least joining the army got me the fuck out of Siberia.

It landed me in Transnistria with the 14th Army under the auspicious flag of a peacekeeping mission. I was under the command of a corrupt general who was systematically selling off an arsenal of forty-two thousand pistols, tanks, and surface-to-air missiles abandoned by the Soviet Union close to two decades after the collapse of the communist regime.

There I was, lying on my stomach on the roof of some derelict office building, soaked to the skin from the icy rain that poured down in punishing sheets, gripping the slick barrel of a Lobaev Arms SVLK-14S sniper rifle waiting for a signal from the general. Surrounding me was nothing but half-torn-down buildings, cracked cement, and weeds. It was what passed for an airport in Transnistria. Those with legitimate business usually flew in through Moldova and then hired a car to cross the disputed border. Those with less interest in having their movements tracked flew directly into the territory by private plane, taking advantage of the deserted former military airbase, which was how the Ivanov brothers arrived that day.

My orders were simple: take out the two men who emerged from the plane with a shot each to the head.

I didn't question the order.

Why would I?

An order was an order, even if it came from a bastard crooked officer.

Although I rarely bothered to care, this time I knew the name of my targets. I had overheard the general talking in his office. The targets were Gregor and Damien Ivanov, two powerful players in the arms trade, who were flying in from America. This would be their last deal with the general. They would have over twenty million in untraceable bonds on them, but the general was only supposed to get a small token amount. They reserved the rest for his replacement, a man Gregor and Damien had installed, ousting the stubborn and unpredictable general.

Unpredictable was bad for business.

The Ivanovs did not know the army had discovered their plans. That the general had no intention of going quietly into retirement with a mere few million dollars for his pains.

I had a choice that day.

Do as the general ordered and then take my chances with the next guy, destined to always be the grunt behind the gun, but receiving none of the spoils. Or take out the general, risking a court martial and a life sentence in some godforsaken Russian prison if the Ivanov brothers didn't show proper appreciation for my efforts.

I looked through the sight of my rifle as the door opened and the steps were lowered on the Ivanovs' private plane. Both men appeared at the top. As they descended the stairs, the general disguised his signal to me as a greeting to them. I inhaled a long breath and released it slowly to steady my hand. My finger caressed the trigger.

At the right moment, I fired.

One shot.

Straight through the general's skull.

In appreciation, Gregor and Damien gave me the several million in bonds they had planned to give the general and hired me on the spot.

They trusted me with their most treasured possession — the safety of their family.

Tonight, I had betrayed that trust.

It would never happen again. I would go back to silently watching over Nadia, but never touching. She would move on and find a man worthy of her, and I would do my best not to kill him for touching what deep in my soul I knew should be mine.

At least that had been my intention, and I had kept my vow for three torturous years.

Then everything changed the day of the wedding.

CHAPTER 6

Nadia
Three years later, present day.

THE SILVER ROLLS ROYCE Phantom limousine traveled down Massachusetts Avenue toward Embassy Row. When the towering white limestone columns of St. Nicholas Cathedral came within view, I inhaled a deep breath, bracing myself for what was to come.

Reaching under the voluminous skirt that crowded us all, despite the spacious interior of the limo, Yelena fluffed the crinoline underneath. "I will not have you exit this limo with a wrinkled wedding gown. Remember Princess Di's wedding? That beautiful gown was an absolute disaster with all those creases."

I helped her smooth out the fine tulle over the champagne silk fabric. The couture gown was from Ziad Nakad's Snow Crystal bridal collection. The A-line ball gown was covered in thousands of tiny Swarovski crystals and pearls sewn in intricate ice crystal patterns all over the skirt and bodice. It looked like something the Snow Queen, a favorite Russian fairytale character from my childhood, would wear. The dramatically long French silk tulle veil was equally stunning. Only a delicate, expert hand could have sewn so many crystals on such a sheer fabric.

Through the tinted windows, we glimpsed my brothers and Mikhail, each elegantly attired in a custom Ralph Lauren tuxedo, waiting for us on the steps of the cathedral just below the massive bell tower, where at this moment five bells were ringing out a chorus to hail the arrival of the bride.

What couldn't be seen were the snipers on the roof and the countless men patrolling the cathedral grounds with weapons under their jackets. I had long since stopped believing in the lies my family had told me about their business affairs. While Gregor and Damien weren't completely straightforward about the kind of business they were really in, I at least now knew it was something completely illegal.

The news didn't entirely surprise me. I guess deep down I had always suspected, I just never wanted to face the possibility. It did shock me in how little it bothered me. I guess that was my Russian blood. In Russia, there was a very fine line between legal and illegal with business. Whatever it was, my family certainly would not stop just because I objected, so there really was no point in causing a fuss. Some may call that a passive and weak attitude, but I simply called it being part of a family. Family was family. Blood was blood, and a few skeletons in the closet would not change that.

"My head is spinning. I shouldn't have done that last shot of vodka at the ransom," complained Samara. "I'd kill for a McD's Cafe Mocha right now."

The ransom was a beloved but chaotic Russian tradition that had taken place at Gregor's house earlier today. All the guests were dancing and singing and laughing. They dressed the women in veils, pretending to be the bride to try to *fool* the groom into carrying the wrong woman off to the altar. My brothers handed out ransom gifts of classic Cartier tank watches to all the men and Cartier white gold and diamond tennis bracelets to the women.

Trays of pink, white and silver zefir meringue cookies were passed around along with other sweets like chocolates and gingerbread and lots of champagne. Then of course there was the vodka and countless toasts to the bride and groom's future happiness and a spectacular wedding — that is, if the groom could successfully ransom her from her family and friends with his bribes.

Outside the window, Mikhail restlessly shifted from foot to foot as he checked his watch. He then leaned over to say something to Gregor, who nodded.

"I think the men are getting anxious," I said.

The biggest part of planning this last-minute winter wedding was all the security involved, which had fallen on Mikhail's shoulders. Given my family's unique business, any high-profile event that took us outside the control of one of our properties put us all at risk. They called reinforcements in from Chicago. Dimitri was attending with his new bride, Emma. He had brought along at least twenty-five of his own heavily armed men.

Alarmed at all the intense security measures, I told Gregor we should call off the big elaborate wedding if there was the chance of trouble and just have something small and private at home, but he adamantly refused.

He repeated a favorite proverb of my father's. "Berezhonogo Bog berezhot." *God keeps those safe who keep themselves safe.* So here we were, celebrating a solemn religious sacrament surrounded by semi-automatic weapons. Sometimes I wished I was still that naive girl kept in the dark about her family's secrets.

Yelena leaned over the backseat to look out the same window. "Good. After what Damien did to me last night, he deserves to wait."

Samara reached up and tucked an errant curl back into the intricate bun at the base of her neck. "I want all the dirty details."

Yelena leaned in, a conspiratorial glint to her gaze. "So, you know how we have that huge shower stall in the master bedroom with all the different showerheads? Well, he actually tied several leather straps around the two highest ones and then— "

Yelena stopped and glanced at me. She waved a dismissive hand in front of her face. "You know what, never mind. It's hardly an appropriate story for right before we walk into a church."

A blush crept up my neck and cheeks. I played with a crystal bead on my skirt. With Yelena and Samara back in my life, this past month had been amazing. We'd spent countless hours in my little jewelry shop coming up with plans to go into business together. Samara had this wonderful idea of renting out a larger space in Georgetown, where we could create a boutique to showcase all of our talents. It would have her paintings, Yelena's dress designs, and my jewelry.

Seeing them both so happy with big plans made me feel like my life had been somehow frozen. Like I had spent these last three years holding my breath waiting for something to happen. Out the car window, I caught another glimpse of Mikhail. He looked devastatingly handsome in his fitted tuxedo.

Yelena's cell rang. She picked it up without looking at the screen. "Hello?" She then mouthed to both of us, *It's Damien.*

We could see he was on his cellphone pacing under the bell tower.

Yelena rolled her eyes. "Stop being such a pushy Scorpio, we're coming." She tossed the phone aside and gathered up the wedding skirt, which was pooled between the backseats. "Damien says if we don't stop chattering like schoolgirls, they are going to march down here and drag us out of the limo."

Samara giggled, then hiccupped, the vodka obviously having a drunken effect on her. "I wouldn't put it past Gregor to toss me over his shoulder and carry me up the stairs and over the church threshold." With a conspiratorial wink, she added, "He's done it before."

Yelena gasped. "Oh my God, so has Damien. Seriously, Nadia, what is it with your cavemen brothers?"

I just shrugged, knowing she didn't really want an answer from me. "We should probably go."

Samara grasped both of our hands. "Just one more second. It's hard to believe three years ago we freaking ran to avoid this day and yet here we are! Fate can be a real fickle bitch, but I'm so glad she brought us all back together. I love you girls."

I squeezed her hand, then teased, "You better not let Gregor hear you cursing like that."

We all knew Gregor hated when women cursed. He thought it made them sound coarse and unladylike. He could be such an old-fashioned Neanderthal about some things, especially since he himself cursed a blue streak whenever he pleased.

Samara raised both arms with her palms out. "What? I said freaking, not fuc—"

She was interrupted when the door violently swung open. Gregor's stormy visage appeared as he peered into the limo's interior. He growled, "I warned you."

"Don't you dare!" shouted Yelena.

I cried out at the same time. "Gregor! You'll ruin her wedding dress!"

He ignored us both.

Reaching for her arm, he yanked her out of the limo and onto his shoulder in one smooth move.

Samara pounded on his back "Put me down this instant, you brute!"

Yelena and I scrambled out of the backseat, racing to lift Samara's veil so that it wouldn't drag and tear along the rough and dirty cement and stone staircase. Yelena got there first and quickly scooped up the gossamer fabric before they damaged it, all the while calling out to Damien to control his brother.

I tried to follow, but the heavy navy blue velvet skirt of my bridesmaid dress tripped me up as I took the first few stone steps. I thought for sure I was going to fall to my knees, tearing the dress and ruining the intricate icicle starburst pattern down the front, but a powerful hand at my elbow saved me from certain embarrassment.

I looked up to see Mikhail's intense sapphire blue gaze on me, then looked down to where his warm hand was touching my bare arm. He instantly removed it as if branded.

Lowering my head so he wouldn't see the tears in my eyes, I whispered, "Thank you."

He only nodded in return, saying nothing. Not that I expected him to say anything. It had been three years of this. Three years of stony silences and averted looks. We never spoke about what happened on my eighteenth birthday. In fact, we had barely spoken about anything since that night. It was like a gigantic wall of ice had been erected between us. He was always painfully polite and nothing more.

Before taking another step, I remembered the kokoshnik tiara. Samara couldn't get married without the Ivanov heirloom. It was a traditional Russian fringe tiara in the shape of a sunburst halo made of pink and white diamonds in a platinum setting.

I turned back to the limo, placed a knee on the seat, and then leaned in to reach along the backseat for the thick black leather case. Shimmying out of the limo, I bent over to gather my heavy dragging skirt into my other hand, wanting to avoid another tripping incident. My head shot up when a few feet away, Mikhail grabbed one of the perimeter guards by the neck.

"Did you get a good look, asshole?" he snarled.

The man clawed at Mikhail's grasp as he pleaded, "I'm sorry, sir. It won't happen again."

A good look? What was that supposed to mean? Mikhail turned his head in my direction. His heated gaze radiated anger. Following his eyes, I gasped when I realized my breasts were practically spilling out of the V-neck of my gown. I must have pushed it down with my knee when I partially climbed into the backseat of the limo. With the leather tiara case for cover, I yanked the dress back into place.

Turning his attention back to the ogling guard, he said, "You're goddamn right it won't, or they'll never find your body." Mikhail released his grip and pushed the man away from him. "Get back to your post."

Lowering my head, I hoped to scurry past Mikhail, drawing no more humiliating attention to myself. I wasn't so lucky.

Just as I was almost past him, his stern voice rang out. "Nadia."

I turned my head slightly and looked at him from the corner of my eye.

He crooked his finger and commanded, "Come here."

I glanced wistfully at Samara, Yelena, and the others who were standing under the bell tower laughing at Gregor's antics as he playfully pretended to spank Samara for keeping him waiting. None of them were paying any attention to me. I slowly turned to face Mikhail.

In just a few steps, he crowded me against the side of

the limo. Placing his palm near the roof of the car, he leaned in. "You and I need to have a little talk about what's going to happen today."

I had to force myself to concentrate on what he was saying. Starbursts clouded my eyes as I forgot to breathe. This was the closest we had been in years.

He had always avoided being alone with me in a room and only said the barest number of words possible when it was unavoidable that we speak. That didn't mean I wasn't aware of his presence. He was always there, in the background, watching.

In three years, I had only gotten past the first date with a guy once. Mikhail was worse than my overprotective brothers in scaring away prospective boyfriends. I had no direct proof it was him, but I had my suspicions. Just like I suspected they involved him in chasing away the only guy brave enough to ask for a second and then third date. The evening of our third date, he never arrived. In fact, he had literally disappeared off the face of the earth, not responding to any of my texts, calls, or emails.

I didn't want to date those other men; I wanted to date Mikhail, but he had made it clear that wasn't ever going to happen. The problem was he didn't want me dating anyone else either. Our relationship was at an odd impasse, and the tension had been building for years. Something had to give, and soon.

Mikhail looked down at me, inhaling a slow steady breath as if he were trying to calm himself down. In the soft, even tones one would use for a child, he said, "You are not to leave my sight today. Do you understand me?"

Wait, what?

I was so shocked at his unusual order, I didn't even respond.

Mikhail placed a finger under my chin and lifted my face to meet his gaze. "I'm going to need an answer...."

He paused. It was there, unsaid, hanging between us. *Kroshka.* He had almost uttered the endearment; I was sure of it. It was on the tip of his tongue as if he were used to thinking it.

"I'm perfectly safe. I'll be with my brothers all day."

"Your brothers' attentions are divided. Mine won't be. I mean it, Nadia. There are things happening today that you are not aware of. Dangerous men are here. I don't want you out of my sight."

He was being ridiculous. We were literally traveling with our own private army right now. I sighed. This was silly. I was nervous enough being part of the wedding party. I hated crowds and being even close to the center of attention. The last thing I needed was also being the subject of Mikhail's intense regard all day. He was just nervous because so many of the additional guards were not part of our usual inner circle. That and the fact that as the head of security, it was his job to keep us safe even though we were in the uncontrolled environment of a public church. This was nothing like the tightly controlled parties at Gregor's house.

I shook my head. "You're overreacting. Nothing's going to happen."

"This is not up for discussion. Step out of line, and there will be consequences. Don't test me on this, Nadia."

I opened my mouth to object to his high-handed

command, but at that moment, Yelena called out for me to bring the tiara.

Glaring at Mikhail, I slid out from beneath his arm and hurried to join my friends. He had absolutely no right to dictate orders to me. I wasn't one of his minion guards, and because of him, I wasn't even his girlfriend, so I had no intention of obeying him.

I would later deeply regret my little rebellion.

CHAPTER 7

Nadia

YELENA CAREFULLY PULLED Samara's veil over her tiara as I adjusted her long wedding gown train. All the guests were already waiting inside the cathedral, including my mother. There were no pews so everyone would stand throughout the two-hour ceremony.

Yelena and Damien took their places directly behind the bride and groom. I stood behind them.

Gregor leaned over and gave Samara a kiss on the cheek through her veil. "You look beautiful, malyshka."

Samara squeezed his hand as she said, "Thank you."

He gave her a wink. "Just remember, you're already my wife till death do us part, no matter what you say to this Archbishop today."

I rolled my eyes. So typically possessive of Gregor.

Yelena was right — both of my brothers really were cavemen when it came to the women they loved.

Without looking, I could feel Mikhail's presence next to me.

Speaking of overbearing cavemen....

The dramatic opening strains of Felix Mendelssohn's *Wedding March* filtered from deep inside the cathedral. How ironic that this piece of music was written for Shakespeare's *A Midsummer Night's Dream*, a play filled with miscommunications and delayed love affairs as a result of an unwanted arranged marriage. We processed only to the entrance of the church where we were greeted by the Archbishop, looking regal in head-to-toe embroidered gold robes.

This was the betrothal portion of the ceremony, where Gregor and Samara would exchange rings and receive the blessing of the church. The Archbishop placed his hand over their joined hands and solemnly recited, "The servant of God, Gregor, is betrothed to the handmaid of God, Samara, in the Name of the Father, and of the Son, and of the Holy Spirit."

Both were handed candles, emblematic of the light that would guide them through their marriage. They then allowed us to proceed into the cathedral.

Compared to the bright but chilly February morning outside, it was warm and darkly inviting inside.

Walking into this cathedral always took my breath away. They modeled it after the twelfth century St. Demetrius Cathedral of Vladimir, Russia, so it had all the solemn grandeur that was usually only seen in European cathedrals. Religious icons on the walls glimmered in the candlelight as the soft beams of light illuminated all the gold leaf painting. Saints dressed in jewel-toned robes of emerald, sapphire, and rubies glowered down from staggering heights. The air was rich with spices as incense burned with the musk scent of frankincense, the sweetness of myrrh, and just a hint of earthy sandalwood.

The Archbishop led Gregor and Samara to the center of the church where there was a small platform covered in a beautiful rose silk fabric that had been embroidered with tiny chamomile flowers — the national flower of Russia — which symbolized the fulfillment of all their dreams and wishes.

Since it was a long-standing superstition that the first person to step on the cloth would be the head of the household, it was no surprise that Gregor stepped up first and then reached out for Samara's hand. As Samara joined him, Yelena and I both arranged the Swarovski crystal champagne tulle overlay and silk draping of her gown, then took our places behind her.

Although he should have stood closer to Gregor, Mikhail remained by my side. As the Archbishop intoned the litany of prayers over the couple, and they decreed their desire to marry to the congregation, all I could think about was the man standing near me. Not beside me, not with me, but near me, always nearby and watching but never a genuine part of my life.

A frisson of excited energy swept over the guests. It was time for the crowning. Unlike with the exchange of rings in an American ceremony, this was the true moment they became man and wife in the eyes of God. The crowns symbolized how they would be the king and queen of their own domestic kingdom.

Yelena and Damien stepped forward. Both of their faces were calm and thin lipped. This was a serious moment, and they would play a crucial part. Each held one of the heavy, imperial-style crowns over Gregor and Samara's heads. The crowns were fitting for a king and queen, crafted from ornate gold with countless enormous diamonds and an ermine fur trim.

The Archbishop recited Psalm 128. "Blessed are all who fear the Lord, who walk in obedience to him."

Mikhail cleared his throat at the phrase *obedience to him*. My cheeks burned as I stiffened my back, refusing to give him the satisfaction of even a dirty look.

Yelena and Damien continued to hold the crowns over Gregor and Samara's heads as the Archbishop exclaimed, "The servants of God, Gregor and Samara, are crowned in the name of the Father, and of the Son, and of the Holy Spirit."

As Gregor and Samara drank three times from the common cup of wine, Yelena whispered to Damien, "And you wanted to marry in some side room of Dimitri's house, covered in bloody clothes, when we could have all this for our wedding, too."

Damien shook his head and then responded in a harsh whisper, "Don't I get any credit for saving your life that day?"

Yelena shrugged and shot him a saucy smile. "Technically, I'm the one who killed the guy and saved you."

He smiled in return. "Just wait till I get you home tonight, little minx."

The playful exchange made my heart ache. I wanted that. I wanted someone I could banter with and exchange teasing smiles filled with promise. Except not the part about killing a man. I may have accepted my family's business, but that didn't mean I was ready to go all in.

The Archbishop led Gregor and Samara around the ceremonial table three times, followed by Yelena and Damien holding the crowns aloft over their heads, to symbolize their first steps of marriage being guided by God. I cast my eyes down and tilted my head slightly to the right to glimpse Mikhail. It shocked me to see him looking straight at me.

Was he as affected by Gregor and Samara's wedding ceremony as I? From the hard look in his eyes, it was difficult to tell. Mikhail kept his emotions closely in check; it was impossible to know what he was thinking or feeling.

Gregor and Samara blew out their candles as Yelena and Damien lowered the crowns and placed them back on a side table. Everyone cheered as the Archbishop offered his congratulations. The organist played Antonio Vivaldi's *Winter* from his *Four Seasons*, another Russian tradition. The season chosen always corresponded to the month the couple were marrying.

As Gregor and Samara made their way to the front of the church, the crowd surged forward. It was the usual mix of family and friends along with business associates, the political elite, and hangers-on. Some were genuinely happy for the couple, others didn't care, and still others were trying to hide their annoyance at being forced to stand throughout the ceremony.

Quickly the crowd felt more like a mob, as people pushed and jockeyed for a position closer to the couple. As I looked around, I could only see the top of Gregor's head and Samara's tiara. Yelena and Damien were swallowed up by the crowd. Turning, I completely lost sight of Mikhail. One man stepped on my dress, jerking me backwards. A woman scratched my arm with her brooch as she tried to force her way past me. Still another man took advantage of the fray to grab my ass. Before I could cry out, a furious Mikhail removed his hand.

Mikhail's powerful arm wrapped around my waist as he lifted me off the ground, pressed against his side. Shouldering his way through the crowd, he carried me to the darkened nave in an isolated corner of the cathedral. His hand slipped over the golden Russian icons before pulling on a hidden lever. A secret panel slid inward. He grabbed my hand and stepped through the stone-arched doorway first, then guided me into the gloom. The panel slid back in place. We were immediately cast in complete darkness. The clearly unused corridor smelled damp and musty.

"Where are you taking me?"

"This is a safer way out," he tossed over his shoulder. I stumbled slightly in my heels over a loose cobblestone, and he tightened his grip on my hand.

"How do you even know about this passage?"

"It's my job to know."

After several minutes, we came to a dead end. Once more, Mikhail slid his hand over the rough surface of the wall to find some unseen latch. A rusty-sounding spring gave way, and a hidden door popped open. A shaft of light brightened the gloom as fresh cool air rushed into the enclosed space. Mikhail pushed the door open wider and ushered me over the threshold. As I emerged from the darkness, I blinked a few times at the bright winter sunshine until my eyes adjusted. It appeared as though we were at the back of the cathedral, shrouded from view by the large trees and bushes that flanked the white limestone columns.

Then a shadow loomed over me, blocking the sun.

I caught my breath. As handsome as he looked in his tuxedo, there was still something dangerous and untamed about Mikhail, especially in the rare times I found myself alone with him. He had this tense energy about him. As if he were always holding himself back.

I fought to keep my voice even as I said, "The others will wonder where—"

He snatched me around the waist and drew me roughly against his body. Before I could utter a sound, his lips claimed mine. I hadn't forgotten the taste or feel of him. Each night in my dreams, I relived our fateful encounter, which felt like a lifetime ago. Clinging to his shoulders, I surrendered to his firm embrace. His tongue played with mine as he devoured me, heart and soul.

A low groan rumbled in his chest as he deepened the kiss, pushing me against the sun-warmed stone wall of the cathedral. The almost threatening press of his cock against my stomach emboldened me. I shifted my hand till my fingertips were just barely touching his warm skin above the starched collar of his shirt. I had this crazy notion I wanted to lick him there. Wanted to taste the salty tang of his cologne and feel his warmth against the tip of my tongue.

At my slight touch, Mikhail strengthened his hold around my waist, pulling me even closer. His hand then slipped upwards, caressing my skin, till his fingers were buried in my soft curls, gently tugging my head back, opening me further to the demands of his kiss.

Rising on my toes, I pressed myself against him. There hadn't been a day I hadn't ached for this man's touch. That I hadn't lived for the small crumbs he tossed my way: a stolen glance here, the accidental brush of his hand there, the sound of my name on his lips no matter how casually.

His other hand slipped inside the V-neck of my dress to cup my breast. I moaned, praying he would pinch my nipples and cause that slight frisson of pain that only increased my pleasure like the last time we were together.

He roughly broke away from our kiss, ruthlessly pushing me back to arm's length, then took a few steps away, his face averted.

I was being rejected. Again.

Instead of warm and smooth, the stone wall behind my back now felt hard and unforgiving. The chilly February air, which moments ago had been invigorating, was now cold and damp. Crossing my arms over my chest, I rubbed my hands over my exposed shoulders.

Mikhail shrugged out of his jacket and put it on me. It reminded me of the last time he put his jacket on me. He was rejecting me then, too.

I shrugged him off. "I'm fine."

"You're cold."

Even as I fought to contain a tremor, I protested. "No, I'm not. I'm fine."

He swung the jacket around my shoulders and tugged on the lapels. "Goddamn it, stop being so stubborn and put this on."

I tried to break his grasp. "I don't want your jacket. I want nothing from you."

"If you don't stop fighting me on this, kroshka, I'm going to take you over my knee and punish you like the child you are being."

Tears sprang to my eyes. Furious, I swiped at them with the back of my hand. The movement caused the jacket to fall off my shoulder. Mikhail stepped closer and pulled it up, once again glaring at me. I didn't care. I was over caring about him.

"No. You don't get to call me kroshka. You don't get to order me around."

Mikhail's eyes narrowed at my disobedient outburst. His jaw clenched as he took a step closer, arms raised.

I stumbled backwards out of his reach. "Don't you dare touch me! Don't you ever touch me again."

I was done being rejected by Mikhail Volkov. I was done waiting for him. Desperately hoping that one day he would change his mind and allow us to be together. Hoping that he cared for me more than he cared about his honor and loyalty to my brothers.

Three years! For three years, I have been pining after this man, longer if I counted the time when I was just a teenage girl with a crush. In many ways, I was still just that teenage girl with a crush. My life stopped that day in my brother's study, as if I had been holding my breath, waiting and longing for what could never be.

My friends had moved on. They had traveled and had adventures. They were now in love. Samara was married with a baby on the way and on the cusp of a thriving art career. Yelena was scheduling a trip to Paris where she was going to study for her dream career in fashion and where she also planned to design her own couture wedding gown for when she and Damien married.

And what did I have?

A small apartment above a little jewelry shop, both owned by my brothers.

No boyfriend. No grand passion. No exciting adventures.

Mikhail stepped forward again, his intent clear as he reached for me. "Babygirl, we need to talk about—"

Without making the conscious decision to do so, my arm swung out. My open palm slapped him hard across the cheek. The ominous crack of skin on skin seemed to echo around the secluded enclosure. I covered my mouth with my hand, stifling a gasp. I couldn't believe I had just hit Mikhail. "Oh my God, Mikhail! I didn't mean to… I'm sorry… I'm just…."

Mikhail stopped and lowered his hands. "No, you're right. I shouldn't have kissed you. I shouldn't have… touched you. I broke my promise to you. I'm sorry, krosh — I'm sorry, Nadia. You have my word, it will never happen again."

My heart broke.

Deep down I had wanted him to protest, to shout and rage. I had wanted him to grab me by the shoulders, pull me close and proclaim that I was his woman, and he would touch me whenever he wanted. With a rueful inward laugh, I realized I wanted what Samara and Yelena had. I wanted a possessive caveman who would defy the world by tossing me over his shoulder and carrying me away. I wanted someone who would fight the odds and my powerful brothers to be with me.

I wanted someone to love me.

I finally realized Mikhail was not that man.

As the tears fell, I shrugged out of his jacket and handed it to him. This time he didn't protest.

It was over.

Although, the bitter irony was, how could something be over that had never really begun? Regardless, it was time to move on. It was time to grow up and leave my silly schoolgirl crush behind.

This time it was he who got to watch me walk away.

It took every fiber of my being, but I refused to glance back.

CHAPTER 8

Mikhail

Just a few more floors... I just needed to keep my shit together for a few more floors.

I inhaled and tried to calm the rising storm deep inside of me. I focused on the off-white illuminated numbers as they switched from the basement parking garage to skip the twenty odd floors to the penthouse as the private elevator picked up speed.

After entering my house, I tossed the keys on a side black marble console. Ignoring the curved French limestone staircase, the carved rosewood moldings and sterling silver accents, I headed straight to the kitchen.

The entire penthouse was expensively furnished with the latest in a sleek, modern style. There were the obligatory paintings of white canvases splashed with bright colors and the occasional vase or coffee-table book on art or photography. Everything was neat and orderly without a scrap of personality. There were no photos from my time in the military or shadow boxes of all my medals or a folded flag from a fallen comrade. No books or CDs. Nothing to give away even the slightest hint about my life.

It was empty, cold, and utilitarian, just like my life.

Opening the refrigerator, I pulled out a Nevskoe Imperial beer and tore through the gold foil-wrapped top. I tossed the metal cap into the sink and walked over to the wall of floor-to-ceiling windows overlooking the Georgetown waterfront and Potomac River. It was a magnificent view, one I rarely appreciated.

Looking out over the early morning winter gloom, I found the dark river still with only an occasional ripple on its glassy surface. Tiny glimmering lights shut off one by one, as the various college bars and pubs along M Street closed for the night. It was that strange ethereal time of day, no longer evening but not quite dawn.

I took a long swig of beer. The cold sting of the bitter hops matched my mood.

Taking a step back, I raised my arm and threw the still full bottle straight at the window. Brown shards of glass cascaded down onto the polished oak floor as thick foam coated the starburst cracks in the window before slithering down to pool in an amber puddle at my feet.

I'd lost her today.

The woman I thought about every waking moment, obsessing over her happiness and safety. The woman I couldn't imagine not being in my life, even if it meant watching from the outside in. The woman I loved.

She was gone.

She was never really mine to lose, but that didn't stop me from discouraging any man who tried from dating her. Like a selfish bastard, I refused to claim her as my own, but also refused to allow anyone else the privilege. I even went so far as to threaten to kill the one man who dared ask her on a third date, making him leave the District and never contact her again.

I had forced her to live in this perpetual space of suspended affection. Treating her like a possession too treasured to be touched, too vulnerable not to be locked away behind high walls and armed guards I controlled. Fuck, I had even argued against her having her own apartment and leaving the safety of her brother's house, knowing it would lead to more independence and weaken my hold on her.

Today, when we were in that cathedral, watching her brother get married, something inside of me broke. I couldn't help thinking what a beautiful bride Nadia would make. I could imagine her belly swollen with our child. I was seeing a life I knew I shouldn't even dare to want play out before my eyes and, God forgive me, I wanted it. I wanted her.

Unable to resist any longer, I'd seized her to me. Held her in my arms and finally claimed those soft lips which had haunted my dreams. The sound of her moans as she clung to me almost had me tearing at the fastening of my trousers to free my cock. I was a man possessed, ready to tempt hell by fucking her against the sacred walls of a church.

When I forced myself to let go of her, I could see something die within her bright blue eyes. A spark vanished. Hope died. I had done that. I had killed that beautiful light within her eyes.

Then, for the rest of the night, I had to watch as she flirted and danced with one guest after another at the wedding. I knew what she was doing. She was taunting me. Deliberately trying to hurt me as I had hurt her. It had worked. It was all I could do not to pull out my gun and shoot each one of them between the eyes for even daring to look at her, let alone touch her.

It was a relief when she retired to her room early.

We had decided before the wedding that the safest security plan would be to have the immediate family stay at Gregor's home for the rest of the weekend till the even more questionable attendees had returned to their countries. It would not be a great hardship for the family; Gregor owned a twelve-bedroom house. At least I knew Nadia wouldn't dare take her revenge flirtations too far under his roof. For now, she was safely tucked into bed in one of the guest rooms.

Weddings were an excellent cover for making illicit deals. It had always been an Ivanov tradition to conduct such business dealings at these occasions, and Gregor's own wedding would be no exception. Three rival third-world dignitaries had all arrived as guests, intending to bulk up their arsenals against each other. It was because of them and other shady business associates that we'd had to beef up security. It would have been an insult not to invite them to the head of the Ivanov crime family's wedding, but that didn't mean they were wanted guests. The sooner they left, the better.

There was also the unresolved issue with the

Novikoffs. Gregor was worried they may still try to cause trouble, despite a confirmed sighting of their patriarch Egor in Moscow just yesterday. Thankfully, the wedding went off without a hitch.

I turned to get another beer and stopped. Something pricked at the back of my mind.

Safely tucked into bed in a guest room?

Was it possible after an entire evening of deliberately trying to bait me by dancing with other men, she had just slipped off to bed like a good girl?

Fuck.

I slammed my palm against a partially obscured button which controlled a hidden panel in the living room. A sliding door concealed behind the sofa silently opened. When I purchased the penthouse, I made a few modifications to the floor plan. Doing the contract work myself, so there were no permits or witnesses, I had sealed off one of the extra bedrooms. Now the only way to enter the space was through a small doorway I'd cut into the wall behind the sofa. After shoving the furniture aside, I bent low and slipped inside.

I devoted half of the room to a small selection of handguns: a SIG Sauer P220, Para 1911 G.I. Expert, a customized M1911 with suppressor and a Smith & Wesson 629 with a weapon light. For bigger fire power, I had a Glock 17 fitted with a CornerShot system and, of course, a Heckler & Koch MP5K. These were just for quick access. The real stuff, like the Browning M2Hb and Type 69 Rocket Launcher, I kept in a secure but nondescript storage container in Virginia.

The other half of the room was dominated by three

large computer screens. I connected them to an 8Pack OrionX. With an insanely fast processor and state-of-the-art motherboard, the designers had built it to accommodate the high video graphic needs of gamers, which made it ideal for the type of surveillance software I ran. After I entered the thirteen-digit code, the computer hummed to life.

Working off its default protocols, the computer immediately brought up my priority surveillance project: codename Kroshka.

As the screens glowed to life, I scanned the many camera angles.

Her brothers knew of my surveillance. Nadia did not. I was sure she would be madder than hell if she knew we'd been watching over her, even after she'd left her brother's. She'd wanted her independence and having this small apartment gave her a sense of that. But that didn't mean I stopped protecting her. I would never stop protecting her.

I wasn't a complete asshole about it. I had cameras throughout her jewelry store and the back work area, and the entrance and exits. Beside the front street and back parking area. All the security hot spots. Everything else was off limits, including her entire apartment. Although even with those limited camera angles, I still had learned a great deal about her.

How she curled up in a ball like a little kitten whenever she fell asleep on that beat-up old secondhand sofa next to her workbench that she loved. How she twirled her hair when she was nervous or trying to concentrate. The way she wrinkled her nose when a piece of jewelry she was working on wasn't cooperating. How she blushed when a customer complimented her designs.

Anxiously, I clicked on the command to shuffle through the various security screens.

All seemed quiet.

Her cellphone was plugged in on the tiny shelf near the cash register.

That meant she was somewhere on property, not at her brother's house like she was supposed to be. The cellphone screen was dark. Since she usually played music on it whenever she was home or in the jewelry store, I assumed the battery was dead.

I continued to click through the security screens, searching for her. If I didn't set eyes on her, it meant she was up in her apartment. Either way, I was going to head over there and drag her back to her brother's.

Finally, I found her.

She had changed out of her bridesmaid's gown into one of her babydoll dresses with a pair of bright pink Doc Martens. She was alone, tinkering with something at her workbench.

I shifted to the next screen, which showed the outside of her jewelry shop.

I watched as a large SUV with no plates pulled up. Three men dressed all in black got out. Two had ski masks over their faces, and one of them was tucking a handgun into his waistband.

Fuck.

She was completely unaware of the coming danger. Without access to her cellphone and no landline, I had no way to warn her to get out.

I was down in the garage and behind the wheel of my Maserati Levante SUV in less than two minutes. It would take me three excruciating minutes to reach Nadia. Thank God she was only two blocks away on a small side street between M and Prospect. The usual Washington bottleneck traffic would be nonexistent at this early hour in the morning. I also knew no District cop would dare pull me over. They knew my car and were paid well to look the other way.

I hit the steering wheel with my fist.

Goddamn it.

I had been a bastard and a fool. Honor be damned. The time for just standing in the background and watching Nadia from afar was over. I was finally going to claim her as mine.

CHAPTER 9

Nadia

I HAD MADE a complete fool of myself tonight.

I rolled the sterling silver sculpting clay between my palms, warming it. Reaching for a heart mold, I pressed the clay into the thin cookie-cutter-like metal frame. The heel of my boot slipped off the footrest on my stool. My feet felt clunky and heavy in my usual Doc Martens after spending the day in strappy high heels. In my maudlin mood, I took it as a sign I should be leaving my old self behind. I'd worn babydoll dresses and Doc Martens since I was a teenager. Maybe it was time to not only give up my schoolgirl crush but my schoolgirl ways as well.

My schoolgirl crush.

The champagne I'd drunk earlier soured as my stomach twisted into knots.

Did I truly believe Mikhail was just a meaningless crush?

Did it matter what I believed?

Mikhail wasn't going to change his mind about us. He had made the decision long ago without even allowing me a say in the matter.

I shook my head as I closed my hand into a fist and pounded on the sterling silver clay, shoving it into the mold with more force than necessary. Tomorrow I would be sad about the death of my hopes for a relationship with Mikhail, but tonight I was still angry.

He had rejected me—again.

And like an idiot I tried to make him jealous at the party following the wedding. Dancing with any man who asked, drinking champagne, laughing too hard and loud at every comment or joke.

It was a waste of time.

I didn't catch him looking in my direction once.

He didn't care.

I picked up a knife and held it aloft over the heart charm before making deep slash marks. If I wasn't so hurt right now, I'd realize Mikhail had always been brutally honest. He didn't want a relationship with me. His job was more important than what we could potentially have together. It was clear to me now. I'd probably imagined all the heated looks and restrained movements over the years. He probably didn't even give a damn about any of the guys I tried to date, if he noticed at all. That one guy who disappeared probably did so because I bored him to death with talk of movies I liked and jewelry making, not because of anything Mikhail did or said.

I reached for the heated brick and primed my gas torch. As I sparked a flame, I thought again how I had badly flirted with all those men tonight. Even Yelena noticed and pulled me aside to ask if I was having a seizure. Apparently, my attempts at flirting resembled someone in dire need of medical attention. Perfect. I tried to tell her I was finally embracing my inner lioness, a reference to my zodiac sign. She just shook her head and said lionesses don't laugh like hyenas on crack and returned to the dance floor where Damien was waiting with an impatient look on his face.

Reaching to my right, I turned the knob on the light switch to dim the lights low in my work area. I found it easier to monitor the firing of silver charms if I wasn't in bright glaring light.

I was breaking a rule right now. I had dared to leave my brother's house to return to my own apartment to get some work done. Everyone would be furious. I shook my head at how ridiculous that sounded. My family would be angry with me for leaving a party a little early and returning home. That was how stifled and supervised my life was, and I was sick of it.

This jewelry shop was supposed to give me a measure of independence from my family and my brothers' business interests. Technically my brothers owned the stand-alone building that housed both my shop and my apartment, but that was only because of tax issues and shell company nonsense. This business was mine in every other respect, and I was damn proud of it.

I adjusted the gas torch and directed the hot blue flame over the heart in slow sweeping circles. The taupe-colored clay smoked as orange and red flames flashed. The cellulose binder slowly burned away. Eventually, the heart heated to a bright salmon pink. Picking up the piece with a pair of tweezers, I placed it in a small dish of water next to my heat brick. Usually, I loved the moment when a small ball of clay seemingly by magic turned into a piece of metal but not tonight.

Tonight, I was thinking about Mikhail and my family and my life—and how things needed to change. Now, before it was too late. If I didn't do something drastic to break away from my family and Mikhail's hold over me, I'd find myself the spinster aunt looking after my nieces and nephews with no children or husband or independent life of my own.

Impulsively, I reached for my cellphone and brought up my contacts. Massimo Agnello's number shown bright white against the dark view background. Biting my lip and blaming the slight buzz I was still feeling from all the champagne, I texted him.

Busy? Want to come over?

Fuck, that was stupid. What if my number was no longer in his phone? It had been over a year since he asked me out on a date, and I said no because I heard Mikhail's voice in the other room and panicked. He probably didn't even have my number saved in his phone anymore. Fuck, it was crazy early in the morning. He was probably sleeping or worse, with someone. This was so stupid. I didn't want to meet up with Massimo. No matter how hard I tried to convince myself I was over him, I still wanted Mikhail. I still loved Mikhail.

Sorry, this is Nadia. Ignore my text. I'm a little drunk and—

The screen went black. My phone died.

Great, I rolled my eyes as I stomped over to the cashier counter and plugged my phone in. Since it was ages old and way past an upgrade, I knew it would take forever to charge, so I wouldn't even know if Massimo saw my text or his response for at least twenty minutes.

Returning to my workbench, I pulled the charm out of the water and reached for the old and scuffed hairdryer I kept plugged in nearby. For larger pieces the sterling silver would need to cool overnight, but this charm was small enough to use a hairdryer. Over the loud hum of the hairdryer, I thought I heard a dull thump. Turning off the hairdryer, I looked around but all was quiet and still in my shop. It was then I noticed the rather ostentatious black SUV which had just parked out in front. The thud must have been the car door.

My heart seized.

Had Gregor or Damien— or worse, Mikhail — noticed I had lied about going upstairs to bed and actually come to drag me back?

I breathed a sigh of relief. They had numerous cars, but I knew them all, and this particular SUV wasn't one of them. Considering the extremely late — or early depending on perspective — hour, it was reasonable to think I had gotten away with my little rebellion. They probably all believed I was safely tucked up in bed. There would be hell to pay tomorrow, but I would worry about that later.

Without another thought, I returned to my work. Setting the hairdryer aside, I picked up a piece of extra fine sandpaper and gently sanded the slightly clouded charm till it had a bright silver shine. With a start, I stared down at the charm as if it had been made by someone else's hand instead of my own. The small heart was perfectly formed and very pretty, except for the angry jagged line straight down the middle.

I had created a broken heart.

My head jerked to the side as I heard two more loud thuds. Two more men got out of the SUV. These men had dark ski masks covering their faces.

Oh God!

I stood up and started to back away as I scanned my workbench looking for a weapon. I reached for a small blade I used for fine etching and my butane torch, but on second thought, I put the torch down. I didn't want to accidentally burn down my own beloved shop. I picked up a heavy hammer I used to achieve the pounded metal look on some charms.

I glanced to the left where my phone was still plugged in several steps away. Where I was near the workbench, I was still in the shadows, but if I dared to reach for the phone, I would be visible inside the shop because of the bluish white glow from the streetlamps outside.

Did I dare?

Maybe they weren't here for me? Maybe they would keep walking?

The men approached the glass door of my shop. One of them shielded his eyes and pressed his forehead against the glass, peering inside.

I held my breath as my grip on the metal blade turned sweaty.

Was I in shadow enough? I had dimmed the light over

my workbench but there was still a soft glow. Maybe he wouldn't see anything worth stealing and move on. I emptied all the glass cases of any jewelry at the end of each night so there was nothing of value visible.

Nothing of value except for me.

My brothers repeatedly used the threat of my being kidnapped as leverage to get me to abide by their strict rules. They even tried to get me to accept additional security and surveillance equipment at my shop and apartment, but I refused, not wanting to live my life under constant watch and desperately needing at least a little bit of independence.

Hindsight being twenty/twenty, I realized how stupid and naïve I was being. It wasn't like I didn't know that kidnapping was a real possibility. My own best friends had experienced it. Yet, it still didn't seem possible. I was the Ivanov brothers' *invisible* little sister. A nobody. Who would want to kidnap me?

The man peering inside stepped back.

I breathed a sigh of relief.

Thank God. They were leaving.

The man raised his arm, and that is when I saw the crowbar.

The sound of shattering glass was muffled by my terrified scream.

CHAPTER 10

Mikhail

Time slowed. I could feel every pump of blood in my veins, every breath of oxygen in my lungs. Each and every nerve ending was sensitized. As I raced through the half empty streets of D.C., nothing escaped my notice. Every flickering light, every dark doorway, every laughing bar patron. I tried over and over to call her cell, but it kept going to voicemail. Every fiber of my being was primed and ready for a fight.

I hadn't felt this much on high alert since my days in the Russian army, when my life was in the hands of sadistic, cold-hearted officers who didn't give a fuck if I came out of a sniper mission dead or alive. Being expendable had a way of energizing a person's desire to survive, just so they could have the satisfaction of saying fuck you to the person who sent them into hell, not caring if they returned, but not this time. This time it was stone icy fear that spurred me on.

I had seen firsthand the types of sick retribution some of the animals we did business with could do to a person. The fact that Nadia was a woman would only make it worse. I didn't see the road ahead of me. The traffic lights, occasional cars, and street lines all faded to black. Instead, I saw her pinned down getting raped by several men taking turns. I saw a knife cutting into her beautiful pale skin as her mouth opened on a gut-wrenching scream. And worse, a vision of her lifeless body on the floor of her beloved jewelry store.

Then, as earlier, other visions flashed across my mind's eye. I saw Nadia in a wedding dress, then lying next to me in bed, then holding our child, then laughing at something over breakfast. Those excruciating three minutes it took me to reach her apartment tortured me with both futures, and I would beat back the Devil himself to make sure it was the latter that prevailed.

Seeing the SUV still parked in front of her store up ahead, I hung a quick right on the street before hers, then left down the alley. That these assholes pulled up to the front told me they were either brazen as fuck or stupid as fuck. That was the problem. I could deal with an experienced hit team, or a couple of expendable rent-a-thug nobodies. Idiots were unpredictable and therefore more dangerous. Kicking down the front door guns blazing was not an option. It was a good way to get shot, and then I'd be useless in saving Nadia. It would be better to enter from the back alley door. As much as I wanted to kick down the door, I took a deep breath and used my key, not wanting to arouse anyone to my presence.

Despite my raging emotions right now, I needed to play this smart. There had been no time to alert my team or her brothers. Besides, they wouldn't get here in time anyway. It was up to me, and me alone, to save her, and when it was three against one, the element of surprise was my only asset.

I silently navigated around the piles of old typewriters she used for her jewelry designs, which littered the back workspace, as I listened for sounds of movement or a struggle. First there was the high-pitched sound of shattering glass, then my gut twisted as Nadia screamed in terror.

Racing to the front, I was just in time to see her struggling against the grip of one of the men. His arm was low around her upper arms, pinning them down. He was dragging her backwards as she struggled to break his grasp. The store was completely trashed. Shattered glass littered the floor as they had knocked several display cases over. My girl had put up a fight.

The man holding her exclaimed to the other two, "Help me with this bitch!"

I leapt over the counter that separated us and slid my arm around his neck, crushing his windpipe. He dropped Nadia. Her small body crumpled to the floor. Pressing her hand to her throat, she looked up at me. My jaw locked when I saw her wide-eyed frightened stare and the bloody scrapes on her hands and knees.

They would pay for that.

With a vicious twist of my hands, I broke the man's neck. He fell to the floor, dead. I reached for Nadia.

Looking behind me, she called out a warning. "Mikhail!"

Crouching low, I turned in time for the second man's swinging arm to miss. After two quick punches to his kidneys, I rose to my full height and used my elbow to dislocate the man's jaw. As he shifted back on his heels from the blow, I gave him a punch to the gut and a final uppercut. He took out several shelves of necklaces as he fell back against the wall before crumpling to the ground, unmoving. Grabbing the gun from his belt, I pulled the slide release back on his Glock, aimed and pulled the trigger, shooting him straight between the eyes.

I turned to Nadia.

I wasn't successful in quelling my rage when she shimmied backwards, shying away from me. She had never seen me kill a man in cold blood, and now she had just seen me do it twice. Still, the thought of her frightened of me caused an irrational burst of anger.

She was looking at me as if I were no better than those monsters who just attacked her.

She was right. I wasn't any better, not really. The Ivanovs may have a strict policy about never going after women and children to seek revenge against a man, but that didn't mean I hadn't done my fair share of despicable things. I couldn't be the head of security for one of the most dangerous crime families on the East Coast and not get blood on my hands. I guess it was foolish to hope she would never learn the actual truth. The problem was, we didn't have time for any of that right now. She needed to trust me. I couldn't have her hesitating or cringing away from my touch.

I snatched her by the upper arm and growled, "Don't you ever pull away from me. Do you hear me, Nadia? Let's go."

Just then, the third man appeared. He must have come from her upstairs apartment. He had stupidly lifted the ski mask partially off his face. I didn't recognize him.

In the time it took to race over here, I had gone through all the possible scenarios of who would be stupid enough to make the extremely dangerous move of going after Nadia to get to the Ivanovs, on the night of Gregor's wedding no less. There were several candidates, anyone from a client to someone closer to home, like the Novikoffs. The Ivanovs had a great deal of enemies. Either way, no matter who it was, it meant a death sentence for them and anyone close to them. Going after Nadia? Their little sister? And a woman? No, that was forbidden. All bets were now off. They had crossed a fucking dangerous line. The Ivanovs and I would instigate a scorched-earth retribution for this night.

The man twisted his head, brushing his ear on his shoulder, before rubbing the tattered sleeve of his shirt under his nose. He then pointed his Glock at me. "Look, Mikhail, I don't want any trouble. Just hand over the girl, all right?"

I pushed Nadia behind me. I now knew two things about the man. One, judging by his twitchy mannerisms and hollow-cheeked, dark-eyed look, he had a nasty coke habit, and it had been at least a few hours since his last fix.

Two, he knew my name. It meant this definitely wasn't a random crime.

I tried to edge Nadia back closer to the front door. If I could keep Twitchy here distracted, maybe she could escape. "If you know my name, then you know what a mistake you just made by pointing a gun at me."

He sniffed again. "I'm not looking for trouble. I just want the girl."

My mouth twisted into a sadistic grin. "Over my dead body."

He gripped the slide release on the Glock and pulled it back, racking a bullet in the chamber. He ran his sleeve under his nose again, inhaling loudly. He then turned the gun to the side, like an idiot in a gangster movie, before saying, "Whatever, man. Your choice."

Three things now. He obviously wasn't trained, or he'd know how to hold a fucking gun, which means his aim was probably shit even at this close range. Anyone with half a brain knew holding a gun at that angle weakened your grip on it, which increased the chance of a harsher recoil that would dramatically affect the accuracy since the gun would kick to the side not up.

"Who hired you?" I asked, fairly certain this coked-out flunky was just a foot soldier and probably not privy to the details of who was really behind this power play against the Ivanovs.

He rubbed his ear on his shoulder again. "I don't know, man. I'm just following orders. This is just a payday."

My eyes narrowed. "Nadia is my property. You tried to take what's mine. Let me show you what happens when someone tries to steal from me."

I could feel Nadia tense against my back.

That's right, my property.

Mine.

She might as well know it all now.

Things had changed.

I was done denying what I felt for her.

She was mine, and no one was going to fucking take her from me.

Reaching my arm behind me, I placed a reassuring hand on her hip. "Close your eyes, baby."

Her hands fisted into my tuxedo shirt as she buried her face against my back.

With my other arm, I struck out, slamming the edge of my palm against the top of the assailant's wrist, knocking the gun from his grasp. I caught it mid-air, flipped it around, and fired, hitting him in the throat. He staggered back, both hands trying to stem the flow of crimson blood that poured from his jugular. He then pitched forward before slipping in his own blood and falling to the ground where he would bleed to death inside of two minutes.

I flipped around to embrace Nadia, holding her close, blocking her view of the dying man and thanking God and all that was holy that she was still alive. I would have lost my damn mind if I had arrived too late.

As I caressed her hair, I whispered against the top of her head, "What the hell were you thinking, kroshka? Leaving the safety of your brother's house telling no one, *without even telling me?*"

I deliberately tried to soften my voice. She already looked unsteady on her feet and facing the full force of my anger would not help the situation.

She stayed silent.

"Answer me," I commanded.

She shrugged her small shoulders. She looked as fragile as a bird in that moment.

I muffled her voice against my chest as she rambled, "I honestly don't know. I just couldn't bear to be in that house. Everyone was so happy. I said I was going upstairs, but I caught a ride back into Georgetown with one of the departing guests, an old friend from high school. I didn't think it would be a big deal. I just needed space. I—"

That explained it. In our world, I had to walk a fine line when it came to security at events like a wedding. I had to have enough security there as a show of force and power, but not so much the normal guests felt uncomfortable or worse, the criminal guests felt insulted at my presumption of violence. Even after all the years that had passed, I was still amazed at how easily the ego of a third-world warlord got bruised. So Gregor's house was guarded during the party, but certainly not to the point where guests leaving were questioned or searched. She probably blended in and one of the new extra guards, who was not familiar with who she was, just let her pass right through the gate.

Now was not the time to yell at her. I did not know if there were more hired hitters waiting outside. I reached out to run the back of my hand down her soft cheek. I leaned down to look her straight in the eye, wanting to make sure she heard me and understood. "We have to get out of here. You do exactly as I say when I say it, no questions asked."

She nodded in response.

I grabbed her by the hand and headed to the back. Leaning down, I reached under her workbench and grabbed up the Bushmaster AR-15 rifle I had hidden there. I ignored her indignant exclamation when she saw the fire power I had secreted into her shop without her knowledge. If I had learned one thing in the Russian Army, it was to always be prepared. As we neared the back area, the heavy thud of a car door slamming was just on the other side of the exit door. I pushed Nadia against the wall and raised my finger to my lips to signal I needed her to be quiet.

"It's probably Massimo," she whispered.

Who the fuck was Massimo?

CHAPTER 11

Mikhail

With the rifle butt braced against my shoulder, I ordered, "When I give the signal, open the door and then stay behind it."

She nodded. Her hand trembled as she reached for the knob, but she took a deep breath and waited for my signal. I was so proud of my babygirl. She was showing her Ivanov blood. She was obviously terrified, but still a fighter.

The moment she swung the door open, I stepped over the threshold and out into the predawn light, gun drawn.

Despite the odd hour, the man was fully dressed in an expensive, tailored suit. He had the tanned, swarthy complexion of an Italian with the black hair and dark eyes to match. He also seemed completely unshaken at having an AR-15 pointed inches away from his face, which spoke volumes.

There was a metallic click, and I didn't need to look down to know he had pulled a handgun on me. Not like I needed a reason to kill him, but he just made it easier.

"No, Massimo!" Nadia cried out as she ignored my explicit order to stay safely behind the door. "It's okay!"

Casually ignoring the barrel of my gun now pointed squarely at his chest, Massimo looked past my shoulder to Nadia. "Dolcezza, are you okay?"

Dolcezza.

My Italian was not great, but I was fairly certain he either just called her sweetness or sweetheart. My chest tightened as I sized up the man who presumed such a familiarity with *my girl*. My anger boiled over when Nadia hastened to assure him I wasn't the threat.

Casting a nervous glance in my direction, she waved off his concern. "I'm fine. He's with me."

Massimo lowered his gun and placed it back inside a hidden shoulder holster under his suit jacket. It was a power play, and more of an insult to me than him actually trying to diffuse the tension of the situation. "When you texted and said come over, I thought you were alone. I did not know you had a *friend* visiting. Should I come back later?"

I recognized him now. Massimo Agnello. His family had carved out a vast territory along the east coast and southern states. They mostly controlled the ports, an extremely lucrative proposition when there were countless criminal enterprises trying to smuggle endless kinds of contraband into the states, including the Ivanovs. He was in my employ last year as a show of good faith, while the Ivanovs and Agnellos worked out a deal. We sent over a cousin of Nadia's, and they sent over Massimo.

He had only been a guard under Gregor's roof for maybe eight months. How the hell did he establish a relationship with Nadia without my noticing? More importantly, Nadia had reached out to *this* man? Tonight? After she had finally decided to move on from me.

My upper lip curled. "That won't be necessary. She's with *me* now."

Massimo's gaze wandered over Nadia. It was clear he noticed the bloody knees from when she fell to the floor on some shattered glass. His voice held just a hint of an Italian accent. "Yes, I can see what good care you are taking of her."

I lowered the rifle and took a step forward. Fuck the gun. I was going to beat this bastard to death with my fists.

Nadia placed a restraining hand on my upper arm. "I'm sorry, Massimo. My plans have changed."

You're goddamn right they have.

"That's fine, another time." Massimo shrugged with a knowing look in my direction. Still, he dared to lean in and whisper to Nadia. "Are you sure you're okay?"

The man was playing with fire.

Then Nadia did the worst possible thing she could do in that moment.

She stepped away from me and touched him. "Thank you so much for ask—"

I didn't even try to contain the territorial feral growl

that rumbled from deep inside my chest and stopped her cold.

Immediately, she lifted her hand off Massimo's arm. She nervously stammered as she stepped back to retreat once more to my side, "Yes... yes... I'm fine."

Too late, little girl.

I was already thinking up punishments.

Wrapping my arm around her waist, I pulled her possessively close.

My message to Massimo was clear. *Back the fuck off.*

I didn't know if he or the Agnello family were involved in this mess. There was no reason to believe they were, but I wasn't taking any chances. I didn't give a damn what his relationship was to Nadia. As far as I was concerned, it was over.

He inclined his head. With a smile and wink in Nadia's direction, he returned to his car and backed out of the alley.

Leaning down, I gave her my only warning. "Now you really are in trouble, kroshka."

* * *

Before I dealt with Nadia, I needed to send a message to Gregor. I punched his number into my phone. I only used burner phones, switched out every few days. All the numbers I needed to know, I had memorized. My call went straight to voicemail, as I expected. Gregor was probably occupied at the moment. It was, after all, still his wedding night.

"It's Mikhail. Someone just crossed a fucking line.

They went after Nadia. I'm taking her to a safe house till I can confirm yours is secure. We cannot trust any of the additional guards, not even the ones Dimitri brought in. We will need a cleanup crew at her store."

I then called Damien and left the same message. Finally, I got ahold of Ilya. He was paid extremely well to always answer his phone no matter the hour. I trusted him to do his job, but only that. Without telling him the true nature of the situation, I instructed him to run a Red Alert protocol on the property's security and wake up both Gregor and Damien. They would listen to my message and get someone to take care of the mess I just left behind. They would understand my priority would be to secure their sister.

Ignoring Nadia's startled reaction to my messages, I took the phone in my hand and smashed it against the nearest brick wall, destroying it. Plastic shards pierced my palm. I welcomed the calming sting of pain.

"Mikhail, listen," Nadia started.

"Don't speak," I warned through clenched teeth.

Logic, discipline, and cold hard reason, my only constant companions my entire life, deserted me. I knew I had no real reason to be angry at her for turning to someone else for companionship. I had denied her for years.

But dammit, I didn't care.

She had turned to another man.

Opening the passenger door to my Maserati, I quickly searched the surroundings. The alley was deserted, with no other sign of activity or disturbances.

I stopped Nadia just as she was about to climb in,

caging her in between my body and the door. "You disobeyed me."

She threw her arms into the air in frustration. "How many times do I have to tell you, you don't own me? You have no authority over me! Are you even going to tell me who the fuck those men were who just tried to kill me?"

"Don't curse."

Her mouth dropped open. She blinked several times before even responding. "Are you serious? Are you seriously admonishing me about cursing when there are three dead bodies inside my store right now?"

"That is not what is important. What is important is you disobeyed my direct order. You knew the family was to stay at your brother's for the weekend. This was a matter of family business."

I was aware she at least had a cursory idea of what her family business really was. She certainly now understood the reason for all the men with guns patrolling her home since her childhood. She knew the dangerous men her brothers dealt with and the reason for my safety protocols, especially during the wedding. Hell, she couldn't have forgotten the dangers her two close girlfriends had faced recently after disobeying her brothers.

"Mikhail—"

I continued as I towered over her, using my considerable height deliberately to intimidate her. "An order given for your own safety and the safety of your family."

She crossed her arms over her chest. "Poshel na khuy. I don't care about your orders, and I really don't care about the *family* business. I'm sick of it ruining my life!"

"*Fuck you?* Remember what happened the last time you

dared to say that to me, kroshka?" I threatened as I watched her beautiful blue eyes widen in alarm.

Grabbing her by the back of the neck, I twisted her around and bent her over the leather front passenger seat of the car. The back of her short dress rose up to the top of her thighs. Her pale slim legs were visible down to her pink Doc Martens.

"Mikhail! What are you doing?" Nadia tried to rise, but my hand on the back of her neck prevented any further movement.

"Teaching you a lesson."

Using my free hand, I flipped up the hem of her dress. I gazed down at the delicate curve of her ass, which was covered in a pair of pale pink silk panties. Gripping the fabric, I crushed it in my hand till it gathered and bunched along the seam of her ass, exposing her creamy skin.

Ignoring Nadia's startled cry, I pulled up on the panties, knowing the fabric would pull taut over her pussy and cause just the slightest sting of pain between her ass cheeks.

"Ow! Stop it! Let me up!"

I released the fabric, confident it would stay wedged like a thong deep between her cheeks. I brought one open palm down on her right cheek.

Nadia screamed, but I knew the interior of the car would muffle her cries.

I couldn't resist shifting my hips forward, rubbing my cock against her exposed soft curves, pinning her to the front seat as I watched one perfect red handprint form. Something deep within me snarled and roared to life, a primal need to devour, to claim. A beast that had just caught the scent of blood and was now hot on the trail of its prey.

Raising my hand a second time, I brought my palm down on the same cheek again and again.

Her small legs kicked out defensively as I continued to spank her ass, alternating between the left and right cheeks. I also punished the tops of her thighs and that perfect spot just below the under curve of her bottom with the cute freckle.

"Stop! It hurts! Please! Mikhail, please!" she cried.

Her pleas only made me punish her harder.

I didn't stop till her bottom glowed a beautiful bright red. Releasing my grip on her neck and hair, I placed both hands on her ass. My skin appeared swarthy compared to her mix of creamy white and cherry red skin. She was so small my hands easily spanned her ass and hips. The heat of her punished skin warmed my palms. My already painfully hard cock twitched. Knowing now was not the time to allow myself to fuck her finally, I couldn't resist pulling her cheeks open. Moving the bunched fabric of her panties aside, I looked at her perfect little rosebud. With the tip of my right index finger, I caressed the puckered skin, pleased when her body jerked in reaction as her hips raised up, a futile effort to evade my intimate touch.

"Please stop," she whined.

Finally, taking pity on her, I pulled her panties free and smoothed the wrinkled silk over her ass cheeks. Nadia hissed the moment the fabric covered her reddened skin. Taking her by the shoulders, I forced her to stand up and face me.

Her soft cheeks were streaked with tears. Her bright eyes darkened with pain. Spanning both my hands along her jaw, I tilted her head back, forcing her to meet my eyes.

"Say you're sorry," I ordered gruffly. I had never been into the spanking kink, but there was something about Nadia which demanded it. She was just so small and vulnerable, practically begging for some man to come and take charge, to dominate her.

I was that man.

I was the only one she would turn to from now on.

I was in charge now.

She would be under my complete control whether or not she liked it.

Her lips thinned to a stubborn line.

"Say it," I growled.

She sniffed and crossed her arms. "Why? I did nothing wrong. I have a right to sleep wherever and with whoever I want."

"Because, *kroshka*, from this moment forward, you're mine. And you will obey me or face the consequences."

"But—"

My grip on her jaw tightened. "This isn't optional. Now say it."

She bit her lip. There was a long pause. Just as I was about to bend her back over the front seat and give her another reminder of what I meant by consequences, she capitulated.

"Okay! *Prosti*," she whispered.

"Good girl. Now let's get out of here."

CHAPTER 12

Nadia

I COULDN'T FOCUS. I knew I desperately needed to think about all that had happened, but right now all I could keep thinking was that Mikhail had spanked me.

Mikhail. Spanked. Me.

Trying not to draw attention to myself, I shifted slightly in my seat. I glanced at Mikhail's profile from under my eyelashes, and my cheeks burned as his lips lifted in a knowing smirk. Damn him. He knew I was squirming because my ass still burned and tingled from his punishment.

Mikhail. Spanked. Me.

Sure, he had spanked me a few years ago that fateful night, but it was nothing like this. Then, it was just a few swats and had felt illicit and sexy. This time was a full-on *punishment*.

Nothing about this morning seemed real. I watched through the passenger window, the various storefronts and houses flying by as we crisscrossed neighborhoods. I didn't dare ask where we were going. I had seen enough cop shows and thrillers to know he was probably trying to determine if someone was tailing us. He was too smart to take me directly to wherever this safe house was.

Nervously, I twisted the hem of my dress between my hands. The small burn holes from the welding torch I was using earlier on a stainless steel necklace caught my attention. I scraped at their curled dark edges with my fingernail.

Mikhail remained silent. The radio wasn't even on.

I had to say something. I should tell him I wanted to go straight to my brothers. The problem was I didn't have the courage to break the silence. Not for the first time, I wished I had Samara's confidence or Yelena's brashness. Neither of them would have allowed a man to bend them over and spank them like a naughty child!

Mikhail moved suddenly, breaking into my thoughts.

His arm stretched out in front of me, brushing my breasts. My cheeks flamed hotter. It was like I was some ingenue who had never been kissed. Actually, that was pretty close to the truth. I had to admit I liked the idea that Mikhail was obviously jealous of Massimo. It was wrong of me to let him think Massimo and I had slept together, but he deserved it.

At night, I dreamed of being the type of woman Mikhail would find attractive. I bet he went for the sexy femme fatale type. Tall and blonde. The kind of woman who men noticed. I imagined her leaning against a bar, taking out a cigarette. Of course, she smoked in that super sexy way, just as he appeared with a light. She would say something cool and confident that would make him laugh. I had never seen Mikhail laugh. I had never even seen him smile. The image was bright and clear in my mind, like a movie reel I played over and over. I would never be that kind of woman. No matter how hard I tried.

Without saying a word, he reached for the strap of the seat belt over my right shoulder. He pulled the strap over my body before securing it in the buckle. He then turned his attention back to the road, still without having said one word. Leaving me even more shaken than I was before. This man had the power to rattle me like no other. Even the simple gesture of buckling me into a seat belt sent my pulse racing.

Several minutes later, we pulled into an underground parking garage. I had just caught a view of the muddy grey water of the Potomac before we slipped past two massive automatic iron doors. It seemed to me we had traveled in one big circle and were back in Georgetown, at one of the swanky high-rises along the river.

Mikhail stopped the car and got out. Feeling foolish for doing so, I remained where I was, instinctively knowing not to move until I was told. Mikhail crossed around the back of the car and opened my door. Turning, I tried to unbuckle my seat belt. My hands were shaking so much my fingers felt numb and useless. Shock was setting in.

After a moment, his large warm hand closed over mine. I held my breath. I could feel his body pressing against my shoulder and back as he leaned into the car.

With a flick of his finger, he released the belt clasp. I avoided his gaze as I climbed out.

We walked up to a single silver elevator door. He punched in a long code. Within a moment, the door opened. We stepped inside, and he punched in another security code. The door closed, and we were racing past all the lower floors straight to the penthouse.

He still hadn't said a word.

After unlocking the door, he pushed it open, then placed a hand at my lower back and guided me inside. I couldn't contain my gasp as we walked down the hallway into the main living room area. This looked nothing like the creepy safe houses that were on television. Usually they were rundown motel rooms, or dilapidated houses with half-boarded-up windows in a bad part of town.

This place was gorgeous. Everywhere I looked, there was expensive marble, elegant furniture, and fancy artwork. I was used to living in a nice house. First at my parents, and then when I moved into the massive compound Gregor called a house for a few years right after high school. Of course, that was more of a punishment and an attempt to monitor me after Yelena and Samara ran away. I guess I shouldn't have been surprised my brothers would have an over-the-top luxurious safe house. Unlike me with my Doc Martens, vintage babydoll dresses, and love of thrift store finds, they had expensive tastes.

Looking around me, I could tell it definitely wasn't lived in by anyone. There were no photos or anything personal to give the place a homey feel. It was cold and formal, like a show house with staged furniture. It was also very monochromatic. All creams and tones of beige, not the slightest hint of color or life.

Mikhail led me into the all-white marble kitchen. It was pristine. I almost wanted to turn one of the oven knobs to see if it was real or just a prop. It was a far cry from my tiny apartment kitchen with its dented cookie tins displayed on top of the cabinets and the bowl of half-eaten popcorn still sitting in the sink.

He walked over to the marble top island and opened a drawer. He pulled out a small first aid kit.

Motioning to me, he said, "Get up on the counter."

I gripped the hem of my dress in agitation. "I'm... I'm fine. Really."

Mikhail stepped up to me. He was just so very tall. The top of my head didn't even reach his shoulder! I was barely five foot two, five foot four if my Doc Martens counted. He was easily well over six feet.

He placed a finger under my chin, tilting my head back. "What have I told you about obeying me?"

I unsuccessfully tried to hide the soft whimper that escaped my lips.

In response, Mikhail's thumb grazed my lip. He repeated his command. His voice soft and low this time. "Get up on the counter, Nadia."

Trying to control the quake in my limbs, I shimmied around his enormous form and stepped toward the island countertop. As I stared at it in indecision, his hands wrapped around my waist. He twisted me around and then lifted me high. I tried to hide my wince the moment my still tender ass hit the hard, icy surface.

He had spanked me.

Spanked me.

I was still trying to wrap my mind around that.

It made me feel vulnerable and, I don't know, handled? Controlled but in this weird, overly protective way. This was all just too crazy. My thoughts were interrupted when Mikhail sat down on a chrome bar stool directly in front of me.

I held my breath.

His dark blue eyes captured mine as he once more placed his large warm hands on the tops of my thighs. Slowly, he pushed my legs open. I tried to resist at first, but that only earned a raised eyebrow and him shifting his hands to my inner thighs and applying more force. I bunched the ruffled hem of my dress between my thighs. He opened the first aid kit, raised a small foil packet to his mouth, and tore it open with his strong white teeth.

The tip of my tongue flicked out to wet my lower lip. It was a nervous gesture, one that immediately caught his eye. His razor focus slipped to my mouth. It made me nervous, so my tongue flicked out again. His left hand was still on my thigh, and his fingers tightened. All the air in the room seemed to leave in a rush, leaving me dizzy. After a tense moment, he returned to his task.

Unwrapping the alcohol swab, he turned his attention to my scraped knee.

"It's fine," I said as I tried to pull a portion of the dress hem to cover my knee, but it wouldn't reach.

Mikhail only gave me a look before returning his attention to my knee.

The alcohol swab was cold at first. Then I hissed as it

stung. It was silly since it was just a small scrape, but it still burned.

Mikhail leaned down and pursed his lips. His warm breath was on my skin. I couldn't breathe. He blew on the cut a second time, taking away the pain. It was such a gentle and caring gesture from such a large, taciturn man.

"Let me see your hands," he ordered.

I knew I wasn't allowed to say no. Reluctantly, I untangled my fingers from my crushed hem and held out my hands, palms up. He grasped them both in his own. I marveled at how large and tan they looked compared to my smaller pale hands. While my small stature had always made me self-conscious, my small, nimble fingers were one thing that helped me be such a great jewelry designer.

Mikhail rubbed a fresh alcohol swab over my lower palms. They were reddened but there were no open scrapes, so this time it just felt cool and wet but didn't sting. All the same, he brought my hands close to his mouth and blew on them. How could such a simple, innocuous gesture feel so taboo and sensual?

Mikhail stood. His enormous frame towered over me. Without saying a word, he grasped my hips and pulled me forward till my ass was on the edge of the counter. My thighs were spread open with my knees on either side of his narrow hips. With a jerk, he pulled me forward again, till I could feel the hard press of his trouser zipper through the thin fabric of my dress and panties.

I kept my eyes trained on his white tuxedo shirt.

He placed a finger under my chin and lifted my head. "We need to talk about what happened tonight, and about *your friend*, Massimo."

I didn't know how to respond. Immediately my mind wondered what the consequences would be if I were to refuse to speak to him. I thought back to the feel of his hard hand against my ass as he spanked me right there out in the open. I resisted the urge to squirm, fearing it may give my thoughts away.

His mouth quirked slightly.

My cheeks burned.

He had read my thoughts, I was certain of it. I needed to get out of here. This was all too much. Our kiss earlier. Our fight. Those men attacking me. Me almost dying. Mikhail killing my attackers. His jealousy and my complete lie in implying I had or intended to sleep with Massimo. Him spanking me. It was all too much. Especially knowing half of this was my fault. If I had only just stayed at my brother's tonight. I just wanted to curl up under a blanket somewhere and make the world stop spinning.

I tried to shimmy out from between his arms.

His hands gripped my hips to keep me in place.

I grabbed his wrists and tried to remove his hands. "Let go. I have to go! I have to talk with Gregor and Damien. They're probably worried."

"No, kroshka. They are not. They know you are with me."

I couldn't breathe. I could feel my chest tighten with panic. Him calling me by his pet endearment for me only made it worse. "No! You don't understand. I have to go!"

"Nadia."

I fought him in earnest, my legs kicking out. "Let me go!" I cried out as I tried to push at his chest.

Shifting his grip, Mikhail easily lifted my slight weight off the counter. I had no choice but to wrap my legs around his hips as he swung around. He took several steps out of the kitchen into the living room and dropped me backwards onto the cream-colored sofa.

His body followed.

CHAPTER 13

Nadia

HIS WEIGHT PRESSED between my thighs, pinning me down.

My mouth opened in shock. After regaining my composure, I lifted my arms to push him off. He easily grabbed my slim wrists, securing them in one hand, and stretched them above my head.

"Let me go!" I pleaded.

In desperation, I shifted my hips upwards to dislodge him. That was a mistake. I could feel the hard press of his rigid cock.

I froze.

"Exactly. So, unless you want me to rip those panties off and give you the fucking you richly deserve, I suggest you talk," he threatened.

I burst into tears. "I'm sorry. For real this time. You're

right. I shouldn't have lied about where I would be tonight, and now this complete mess is my fault."

Mikhail made a soothing sound as he stroked my hair with his free hand. He leaned down to kiss the corner of my eye where a tear had escaped. Once more, the gentle gesture struck me, coming from such a fierce-looking man.

"Don't cry, baby. It's not your fault. I'm going to make it all better, you'll see."

I looked into his earnest blue eyes. His words were a strange mix of taboo and calming.

Mikhail shifted, raising his body off me, and I instantly missed the comforting weight. He moved to sit on the other side of the sofa. I swung my legs free and sat up. Just as I was about to settle myself into position, he wrapped his arms around my waist and lifted me onto his lap.

"Mikhail," I protested.

Ignoring me, he pushed my head onto his shoulder.

This new side of Mikhail was difficult to get used to. With our limited relationship, he had always been strictly professional except for those two times he kissed me. Now he was holding me close and kissing my tears away. What was happening?

He continued to stroke my hair and speak soothingly. "I'll have my men grab whatever you need. We'll move you back in with your brother temporarily. Everything's going to be fine."

I stiffened. "I'm not moving."

"What?"

I tried to pull back from his embrace to face him, but

he just tightened his arms. "I'm not moving. I love my apartment and my shop. I'm not about to let whatever illegal activities my brothers are involved in ruin that. I'm sorry about what happened tonight, but that doesn't mean I'm going to uproot my whole life!"

I could feel his body tense. Then he lifted me off his lap, stood abruptly, and started to pace. I was afraid to speak, unsure of what I'd said that had set him off. I watched in silence as he paced like a caged animal. He ran his hand through his dark hair. Finally, he stopped to face me. His eyes looked hard. I could see a muscle in his cheek twitch as he clasped and unclasped his fists.

"If I hadn't arrived in time, they could have killed you — or worse."

The last thing I wanted was to fight with him about this, but I knew if I relented now there would be no turning back. He was just like my brothers. Both he and they would steamroll right over me, till I found myself living under my brother's roof until I was an old maid. I shook my head. "I'm glad you arrived in time. Really, I am. It was amazing. If you hadn't gotten there precisely when you did, I—"

Wait.

How did he manage to get there at just the right time?

How did he even know I was there?

His eyes narrowed. He moved swiftly toward me.

I leaned away, pressing into the cushions of the sofa. He placed his hands on the sofa back and leaned down, his sharp features close to my own. "Don't. I know what you are thinking and don't. Eto bylo dlya vashey zhe zashchity."

"For my own protection?" I slipped out from under his arm and stood. "Have you and my brothers been spying on me?"

He didn't even have the decency to look embarrassed or ashamed.

He crossed his arms over his chest. Through the thin white tuxedo shirt, I could see the splashes of color from the tattoos on his forearms. He had long since abandoned the bow tie. The shirt was open at the collar, exposing a small section of his chest. There were also a few flecks of blood from his fight earlier. Most people probably would have been bothered by that. Knowing someone else's blood was on them, they probably would have torn the shirt off the moment they had gotten the chance. It didn't seem to bother Mikhail. Worse, it barely seemed to bother me. It was like despite being kept away from my family's dark secrets, I had still somehow absorbed all the violence into my soul.

He raised an eyebrow. "You didn't honestly think your brothers would have let you move into that apartment without some assurances about your safety?"

Turning my back on him, I stared out the massive window. The sky was ablaze with color, bright orange, fiery pink, and violet as dawn broke. Seeing the buildings of the Georgetown waterfront, I recognized precisely where Mikhail had taken me. We were less than three blocks from my shop.

There was a large starburst crack in the glass and long hazy streaks of dried liquid. My gaze swept downward to a strange pile of shattered amber glass and a puddle of what looked like beer on the floor. Slowly pivoting, I looked around the room again. My initial reaction to the space was correct. This wasn't a safe house.

My eyes narrowed as I stared at Mikhail. "Whose penthouse is this?"

He ran his hand through his hair. "What does it matter?"

"It's your house, isn't it? I was never really independent at all. You've been nearby the whole time." I paced around the living room. "So do you have some secret room for all the surveillance equipment and computer screens? Is that how you knew I was in danger?"

His eyes flicked to the wall behind me. I hadn't noticed before, but the other sofa was slightly askew. Behind it there was a sliding panel only partially shut, as if someone had been in too much of a hurry to make sure it closed properly. I placed a hand over my mouth and turned back to him with wide eyes. "Are you fucking kidding me? There really is a surveillance room?"

I paced down the center of the room, a habit I'd obviously picked up from him. I wrapped my arms tightly around my middle.

"Kroshka...."

My body whipped around. "Don't call me that! You don't get to call me that ever again!"

"The fuck I don't!" he shouted back as he took a few steps toward me.

I picked up one of the useless pieces of decor he had about the place to make it look like a normal home and not like the security surveillance headquarters it really was.

He raised his arm. Pointing a finger at me, he warned, "Don't you dare!"

I threw it.

He ducked in time for it to smash against the wall behind him.

"Liar!" I cried as I launched another missile, a glass cylinder holding an unlit candle.

He lunged for me. I feigned right then left and bolted to the other side of the room, placing the sofa between us.

"You're a fucking liar! You've been fucking lying to me this whole time!"

"Language!" he roared as he circled around. I kept out of arm's reach, always keeping the length of the sofa between us.

I fired back, purely out of spite, the one phrase I knew would piss him off. "Poshol nahuj!"

Reaching down, he used both hands to shove the sofa. It easily slid across the polished dark bamboo floor, removing the barricade between us. He rose to his full, unbelievably intimidating height. A vein pulsed in his temple as his chest rose and fell with each agitated breath. I had angered the beast. Without the sofa between us, I was vulnerable and unprotected.

"Apparently," Mikhail snarled, "my bad girl needs another lesson from me."

There was only one option left for me. I turned and bolted for the front door.

He was right behind me.

Snatching my arm, he swung me around and used the force of his body to press me against the wall of windows. Behind me was a panorama of stars and the flickering lights from the boats out on the Potomac, a peaceful scene that belied the war brewing between us.

He pressed his fingertips into my upper arms. "Listen to me."

Not wanting to listen to his excuses and lies, I clawed at his grasp, trying to wriggle away.

He shifted his hold to my waist and swooped down to capture my lips in an attempt to subdue me; I shifted my head to the side, avoiding him. It didn't work.

Tightening his hold on my waist, he lifted me high off my feet. I was anchored against the glass by his hips, his hard cock pushing against my stomach. He released his hold and wrapped his hands around my jaw, forcing my head forward. He then took possession of my mouth. When I tried to keep my lips closed, he pressed his thumbs into the soft flesh of my cheeks, forcing my jaw open. At first, I returned his kiss, then I returned to my senses and fought back and bit his lip.

His head reared back. He swept his tongue across his lower lip, lapping up a tiny bead of blood.

He wasn't deterred.

He captured my mouth again. I could taste the metallic tang of his blood. His fingers slipped into my wild strawberry curls, holding my head steady for his continued assault. He pressed his body tighter against my soft curves, refusing to give quarter till I accepted him and accepted his dominance over me.

He broke the kiss and breathed against my mouth. "You're mine. Fucking mine."

I knew the moment the fight left me when I felt the brush of the back of his knuckles down my cheek. Swallowing my capitulating moan, he deepened the kiss. He interlaced his fingers with mine and pressed my hands against the glass on either side of my head. The cold, hard surface brought reality crashing back. I desperately wanted to return to the warmth and ignore all else but knew that was not possible.

Using every ounce of strength I possessed, I pulled back. He ran a thumb over my cheekbone, feeling the soft warmth of my flush. I never wore makeup, but at this moment, I was certain my swollen lips looked as if they were bright with a kiss-smeared crimson lipstick.

"Why?" I whispered, the sting of betrayal bright in my eyes.

He took a deep breath and told me the jaggedly raw truth. "All I can say is, from the moment I met you, there wasn't a doubt in my mind that you were meant to be mine and mine alone. Part of that meant you were mine to protect."

"So you snuck a security camera into my shop?"

His eyes hardened as he shifted his gaze away from mine.

Fuck. It was so much worse than just a single security camera. He and my brothers had probably been watching and monitoring every step I ever made from the moment I left Gregor's house, seeking my so-called independence.

He took a step back and let me slide back onto my feet. From this position, he towered over my slight frame. "Baby, you are just going to have to trust me."

"Trust you? I feel like I don't even know you anymore, if I ever did."

"I never had any cameras in your apartment. Just the entrances and exits and your shop."

I threw my arms into the air. "Oh, well, that makes things all better."

"I will not apologize or feel guilty for doing my fucking job, for wanting to keep the woman I love safe."

I shook my head. "No! No. You can't do that to me. You don't get to say that. You don't get to give me the cold shoulder for three years and then one day announce that we're together and you love me because *you've* finally decided you want me. That's not how this works."

He slammed his fist against the window. The glass vibrated from the impact, and the starburst crack a few feet away lengthened. "Damn it, Nadia. You know why we couldn't be together. It was for your own good."

I shifted away from the window and backed up a few paces, needing space from him. I couldn't think straight when he was that close to me. "*For my own good. For my own protection.* You're no better than my brothers. Deciding what is best for me without even bothering to ask me!"

He started toward me. "I am what is best for you. I've always been what is best for you. Me and me alone."

Picking up the nearest object I could lay my hands on — a blue glass bowl —I shouted back, "Then you should have put a ring on it instead of just standing on the sidelines all these years." I threw the bowl straight at his head and once again bolted for the door.

I didn't make it two steps before he caught up with me. Grasping me from behind, he wrenched my body close to his own. He leaned down to whisper in my ear, "You're not going anywhere."

My hands balled into fists as I stomped my foot, trying to step on his toes and force him to release me. "Let go!"

Mikhail moved so quickly I didn't even have time to protect myself. He spun me around in his embrace. His right hand struck out, wrapping his fist into a shock of my messy curls, then he wrenched my head back. His other hand went to my lower back, pushing me forward and against him. My hands rose to press back against his chest. He didn't budge.

He stormed back, "You need to understand that as of tonight, things have changed. We're together now, and I'm not letting you go."

I twisted my head to the side. "We're not together. All I've ever been to you is a security job."

"You've been a whole lot fucking more to me than some stupid job, Nadia."

His mouth swept down to capture my own.

CHAPTER 14

Mikhail

THIS WASN'T A KISS.

It was an act of possession.

I knew she didn't truly hate me, and she had every right to be angry at me. I was angry at myself. I should never have kept my distance these past years. It had been a mistake, one I was going to rectify right now.

Forcing my tongue past her lips, I tasted and claimed. After swinging around, I pressed her against the wall and pushed my hips into her softness. I wedged my thigh between her legs and raised it high. She was so tiny, I easily lifted her off her feet, forcing her to ride me. Forcing her cunt to rub against the top of my leg. I sucked her bottom lip into my mouth, scraped the sharp edge of my teeth against the soft pink fullness. The feel of her small hands as they pressed against my chest nearly drove me wild. I wanted to feel her cool touch against my own heated skin. I had this crazy notion that perhaps, just maybe, she had the power to tame the demons inside of me. That this tiny slip of a woman might actually be my match.

These past three years, I had kept my obsession in check. Kept it leashed and tamed, as I forced myself to only watch but never allow myself to touch her again. Keeping her safe from my own animal needs. The knowledge that she had been in danger while I watched unknowing from a distance nearly tore my gut to shreds. My anger and fear felt like physical pain, a hot knife digging into me. I didn't know what the fuck was going on, but I knew it would end with me.

I would cross to hell and back to keep her safe.

Never again would I let her leave my side.

My grip on her hair tightened as I deepened the kiss, grinding my cock against her thigh as I forced her to ride my own. I slid my hand between her thighs, feeling the wet silk of her panties. I couldn't contain a growl as I swallowed her own helpless whimper. My baby wanted me as badly as I wanted her. I moved the fabric of her panties aside and slipped a single finger between her slick folds.

Rolling my shoulders, I lowered my head and rested it against her forehead as I took a deep, controlling breath, forcing my pulse to slow, willfully ignoring the spike of pain in my fully erect cock. I looked down into her small, upturned face. Her cheeks were a deep pink and her lips looked bruised and swollen. There was a rush of possessive pride knowing I had marked her as my own.

But it wasn't nearly enough.

Seizing her by the wrist, I didn't even give her a chance to look around. I pulled her into my bedroom. Nadia tried to pull back the moment she realized what room I had brought her to, but I wouldn't let her. The king-size bed was on a platform, dominating the room. Instead of a headboard, it was pushed up against a wall of tinted floor-to-ceiling windows overlooking the river. I only let go of her when she was standing at the foot of the bed. I gave her shoulders a small shove, and she fell back.

Her eyes widened. "What do you think you're doing?"

I took one of her legs in my hand and raised it up high. I worked the laces of her thick Doc Marten boots. Except for the occasional high heels when she was wearing a cocktail dress, I had never seen her wear anything else on her feet.

"Hey!" she protested as she tried to pull her leg out of my grasp.

Pulling the boot free, I tossed it to the side. Despite her attempts to evade me, I snatched up her other leg and made quick work of those laces as well. I left her in a pair of yellow ankle socks with lollipops on them. With her leg stretched high, her dress rode up on her thighs, and I glimpsed her pink panties. The sight just made my already hard cock harder.

I watched as she scrambled to the other end of the bed. With the breaking dawn light from the windows, she was framed in shadow, her wild strawberry blonde curls a halo around her. While I couldn't make out the distinct features of her face, I knew her eyes were on me.

Keeping my gaze trained in her direction, I unbuttoned my shirt and pulled it off my shoulders. As I lowered the zipper on my pants, I kicked off my shoes. Pushing my thumbs into the waistband of both my pants and boxers, I shoved them to the floor. I knew I was both a large and physically fit man. I fisted my hard cock. Although she was in shadow, I could imagine her biting her lip nervously.

She should be nervous.

"Come here," I demanded.

She stayed where she was.

"Rule number one. Never disobey me."

"Rule number one? How many rules are there going to be?" she threw back saucily.

"As many as I want. Now come here."

After a moment's hesitation, she slowly moved to the center of the bed, but no further. She was on her knees, her babydoll dress falling about her in soft folds.

"Take off your dress."

Her pretty pink lips opened on a gasp.

"Now," I barked impatiently as I gave my shaft a hard squeeze.

Her hands flew to the small pearl buttons down the front. One by one she unclasped them. A blue lace bra peeked through her fingers as the dress fell open. When she had unbuttoned the dress to her navel, she slowly let it fall off her shoulders.

The gesture was innocently seductive. Unlike other women I've known in my life, I knew there was no artifice. This was not some practiced move meant to tease. I loved the fact she had on a pair of simple pink silk panties and a blue bra. My girl wasn't some shallow, femme fatale with matching lingerie, practiced in the manipulation of a man. She was beautifully genuine.

"Take off your bra."

"Mikhail, I haven't done...."

My brow furrowed. "Are you telling me you're a virgin?"

The idea stirred my blood even more. I selfishly wanted it to be true. I never wanted to think about her with another man. She was closely watched, but not twenty-four seven. It was possible she wasn't a virgin, if not probable, but for me to hear about any past lovers in this moment would stir my jealousy out of bounds, especially after my encounter with Massimo earlier.

She hesitated, then answered. "No. It's just that I have had little… well… not much practice."

"Stop talking and take off your bra."

Reaching behind her, she unlatched the bra. It fell down her arms, exposing a perfect pair of breasts that matched her petite frame — small with a gentle curve. Her nipples were the same color as her pink lips.

"Now your panties."

Watching her slowly strip off her clothes was driving me insane, but it was an insanity I wanted to savor. I almost blew it on the sofa earlier when I let my cock control my emotions. To take this beautiful creature rough-and-ready style would have been sacrilegious.

Watching as she rose up and rolled the waistband of her panties over her hips and then down her legs, I took a few steps over to the closest bureau. As she curled her legs up, trying to cover both her pussy and breasts, I pulled free a toy I'd purchased with only her in mind.

I'd lost count of the times I had jerked off in this very bed to the thought of using it on her. It was a soft, purple dildo in the shape of a dick, about two inches wide and seven inches long. At the base was a helpful suction cup. Her large blue eyes followed me as I walked past her. After tossing all the pillows out of the way, I reached over and secured the dildo to the large window directly behind the bed.

I liked my sexual play rough and dirty, and couldn't wait to buy toys to fill her every hole. She might as well know that now from the very beginning. Although I wasn't worried. From the way she responded to that erotic spanking I gave her while bent over her brother's desk a few years ago, I had a feeling my baby shared my same dark tastes for pain mixed with pleasure.

Nadia kept her gaze forward. Her body trembled slightly.

"Crawl over to me."

The room was silent except for her slightly erratic breathing.

Nadia shifted on her hip and then onto her knees. Her slight breasts were pressed between her upper arms as she hesitantly shifted one leg forward, then the other. She crawled the short distance to the head of the bed.

She then tilted her head to look up at me, her eyes luminous with fear and desire.

I stroked her cheek with the back of my hand. "You're going to be a good girl and do everything that I say, aren't you?"

Without taking her eyes off me, she nodded.

Fuck. This woman was going to be the death of me.

The very idea of making such an angelic face force fuck a cock got me harder than I even thought possible.

"I want you to open your mouth and suck on the head of the dildo."

Turning back to the window, she shifted her body forward so she could stretch out her neck and take the bulbous tip of the dildo between her lips. I was pleased at her unquestioning obedience.

"Good girl. Swirl your tongue around the tip."

I watched as she obeyed.

"Now I want you to lick the entire shaft, get it nice and wet."

The bright purple silicone of the dildo glistened as the tip of her tongue swept over its slightly bumpy surface.

"Now I want you to try to take it down your throat."

Nadia opened her lips up further but only put about three inches in her mouth.

"I think you're being a bad girl on purpose," I murmured into her ear as I climbed up behind her on the bed, rubbing my cock between her cheeks. Her only response was to whimper.

"Does my bad girl need a spanking to get her to do what I say?"

Without waiting for her response, I raised my right arm and brought my flat palm down hard onto her cheek. I repeated the gesture several more times. I didn't stop till her ass cheek bloomed a bright, angry red.

"It hurts!" Nadia cried out as I shifted my position to grasp her right hip and raise my left arm.

"Obey me. Push that cock down your throat."

She struggled to keep the dildo in her mouth as she started to cry.

Her left ass cheek tensed a moment before I struck. I continued to spank her until both her bottom cheeks were warmed up.

"Please! I'm trying! I can't! I don't know how!"

Fisting her hair, I growled, "Open your mouth wide."

She was so tiny, I could easily see over the top of her head as she obeyed. As soon as her lips closed over the tip, I pushed on the back of her head.

Nadia gagged and struggled as the pliable silicone pushed along her tongue to tease the back of her throat. I eased up the pressure, allowing her to take one breath before I once more pushed on her head, forcing her face onto the cock.

I was training her, of course.

She would find it much easier to deep throat my nine-inch cock later.

Inch by punishing inch, the dildo pushed into her mouth. I relented when she had swallowed at least half.

"Are you my dirty girl?"

Nadia moaned.

I spanked her ass.

"Yes! Yes! I'm your dirty girl."

"You want me to force you to swallow more cock?"

"Yes," she whimpered.

Twisting my hand into her hair, I forced her mouth on the plastic cock a few more times.

Releasing my grip, I told her to keep sucking while I moved to lay flat on the bed. I positioned myself between her thighs, her beautiful cunt just inches from my mouth.

As she sucked on the plastic cock, I tasted her. Using my thumbs, I spread open her folds and flicked her clit with my tongue. Her hips bounced, but I followed her with my mouth, gently scraping the delicate bundle of nerves with my teeth as I pushed two fingers into her gloriously wet hole.

Fuck. She was tight.

I could hear her slurp and choke as she continued to please me by sucking on the dildo.

Pulsing my fingers into her, I continued to rhythmically circle and flick her clit till I could feel her inner thigh muscles begin to clench. Just as she began to crest, I shifted my hands to palm her ass, digging my fingers into her still punishment-warmed skin.

The sound of Nadia crying out with pleasure as she came was the sweetest sound I had ever heard in my life.

Switching positions, I moved to kneel directly behind her. I spread her ass cheeks open so I could see her perfect little puckered hole. With my fingers still slick from her pussy, I circled the pale pink skin, reveling in how her body twitched and trembled in response.

"You know I'm going to hurt you when I stick my big cock in this tiny hole."

Nadia looked at me over her shoulder, "Please, I've never…."

I stroked her smooth back with my other hand. "Don't worry, baby. You'll like it when I make it hurt."

Placing my finger at her tight entrance, I forced it in deep past the second knuckle. Nadia cried out as her knees buckled under her and her hips swung forward.

"Back into position," I commanded.

With a whimper, she pushed herself back onto her knees, "Please, it hurts."

I pumped my finger in and out of her ass. I could feel the ring of muscle tighten then stretch.

Taking pity on her, I said, "I won't fuck your ass today if you swallow all seven inches of that cock like a good girl."

"I can't. It's too big."

"You're going to have to get used to deep throating a cock, babygirl, because I plan to force all nine inches of mine down your small throat every chance I get."

Leaning over her small body, I placed a hand under her jaw, tilted her head back, and playfully bit her exposed neck. Licking the red circular wound, I then whispered into her ear, "I want to hear you choke and gag as you struggle to obey me."

I could feel the vibration of her groan as it rumbled up her slim throat.

"What's it going to be, baby? Do I fuck your ass or do you force that cock down your throat?"

"Please, I'm scared to take your cock in my ass."

She should be. As it was, I was going to tear up her pussy with the thick weight and length of my shaft. Her tight little ass didn't stand a chance.

"Then you know what I want to hear."

"I'll swallow the cock."

"Why?"

"Because I'm your dirty girl."

"Yes, you are," I growled as I gave her shoulder a bite.

Moving back into position, I shifted her forward.

"Open your mouth and suck on the tip."

As she obeyed my command, I rubbed the tip of my cock over her slick folds before placing it at the entrance to her tight pussy.

"Keep that cock in your mouth."

With no further warning, I violently thrust my hips forward. The impact pushed her body forward, forcing her mouth deeper onto the fake cock as I drove my shaft equally deep into her impossibly tight cunt.

Nadia cried out in pain.

I cursed and pulled out. "What the fuck?"

CHAPTER 15

Mikhail

I HAD ASKED her if she was a virgin.

She'd said no.

Why would she say no?

Why would she lie?

While the bastard in me was elated that I was truly her one and would definitely be her only, I couldn't deny the fact I had treated the woman I loved, an innocent virgin, no better than a whore with my rough demands.

I rubbed her back as I pushed aside her hair, wanting to see her face. "Baby, I'm so sorry. I would have never taken you so rough. Jesus. Why didn't you say something? I would have been gentler. I would have taken it slowly."

Her hips rose to rub against my cock. "That's why I said nothing. Gentle isn't us, Mikhail. It never has been."

I stroked her hair. "But… Christ… Nadia, I hurt you. You screamed."

She buried her head in the pillow and responded.

"I can't hear you."

She raised her head slightly, her cheeks bright red. She whispered once more, "I liked it."

My cock hardened again as I ran my hand down her back and over her ass. "You liked it? You liked the pain?"

She buried her head in the pillow again, but nodded.

I smiled. I knew she was the perfect woman for me. Still, the dildo attached to the window caught my eye. I was doing and saying things to her that really weren't appropriate for a virgin. If I had known, I would have initiated her into the more hardcore bedroom play later.

I knelt back up behind her on my knees. Slipping a hand between her legs, I teased her clit, bringing her back to the brink again. "Are you sure about this? I don't want to hurt you but, baby, there is no fucking way I can be gentle now."

She breathed as her own fingertips brushed past mine as she reached for my shaft from between her legs, pulling me closer. "I don't want you to be."

I shook my head. "How the hell do you know… how do you know how to… you're just an innocent… I don't understand how…." I couldn't even finish the sentence. Not five minutes earlier I had watched her try to push a seven-inch dildo down her throat, all while agreeing she was my dirty girl as I spanked her ass, and yet she was a virgin.

Nadia gave me a throaty laugh as her head tilted back. Her strawberry blonde curls teased the creamy skin of her shoulders. "I was a virgin, Mikhail. Not a nun. I have read Fifty Shades, you know, and watched porn."

I fisted her hair and pulled her head further back. Leaning down, I nipped at her ear as my fingers teased her tight entrance. "Oh yeah? Did you like it? Did you dream about me being the one to fuck you hard and fast like that?" I pushed my finger deep inside of her.

"Oh God, yes! Yes!"

Her body trembled beneath my touch. Her orgasm was one of the most beautiful things I've ever witnessed. I would forever remember the sound of her pleasured cries.

Grabbing her hips, I drove into her tight heat. Never in my life had I delayed my gratification for a woman for so long, but now the beast was unleashed. I couldn't stop if the hounds of hell were at my heels.

Her wet heat struggled to stretch around my shaft, and I ran my hand up her back until I could dig my fingers into her tangled hair. I could feel her body brace for what she knew was coming next.

As I thrust forward, burying my cock deep inside her cunt, I pushed against the back of her head. The sounds of her gagging and choking on the silicone cock as I forced it deeper than ever before down her narrow throat just drove me on harder.

Over her head, there was a panoramic view of the Potomac River and the sparkling lights in the windows of a high-rise nearby as I finally took possession of her. The voyeuristic idea of having her exposed to the world but technically still unseen only fed my lust.

Her hands fisted in the bed coverlet as she struggled to breathe.

Still, I thrust harder, moving her head up and down the plastic shaft as my shaft thrust in and out of her body.

Fuck! The sight of her small body swallowing my cock as I forced her to face fuck the fake cock nearly drove me insane. I shifted my hand on her ass, till my thumb could press against her asshole. Applying steady pressure, it popped past her feeble resistance. This time when Nadia tried to move her hips away from the pain, she only succeeded in pushing her own face further onto the dildo.

My balls tightened as I looked down at her vulnerable body being pierced in all three holes, knowing that the only thing occupying her mind was pleasurable pain.

"I'm going to come. Time for you to take that last inch down your throat."

Nadia tried to shake her head but my grip on her hair prevented it. Besides, I would not take no for an answer. She didn't want to be treated like a fragile virgin, so I had no intention of doing so. I was going to fuck her with all the fire, heat, and passion I felt for her.

Pausing my thrusts, I applied steady, unrelenting pressure to the back of her head. I watched as her lips opened around the thick shaft. It was just thick enough to make her struggle, but not so thick it stretched her lips thin. They still looked full and pink as she did as I commanded.

"I want your nose to touch the glass of the window."

I kept pushing. Nadia's body shook with the effort as spittle dripped from the corners of her mouth, soaking the sheets.

Finally, the tip of her pert little nose touched the cold smoothness of the glass.

"Now keep it deep in your throat till I come," I ordered.

Her shoulders shook with the effort to please me.

Keeping my grip on her head, I thrust deeply. Pulling all the way out, only to slam back in. I could feel my orgasm building. The exquisite pressure. I knew I only had a few more seconds before I had to let her go so she could breathe again.

With a cry, I thrust in deep, feeling my balls slap against her swollen pussy. Thick come coated her inner walls as I roared my release. It was the most completely perfect orgasm of my life.

With my cock still buried inside of her, I loosened my grip on her head as I wrapped my arm around her middle. Gently, I pulled her back till I could hear her desperate gurgles and gasps for breath as the long dildo slid out of her throat and past her lips.

I collapsed onto my side, taking her with me.

Shifting my arm, I placed my hand between her legs, searching for her clit with the tip of my finger.

"I'm not done with you yet, kroshka."

CHAPTER 16

Nadia

My dreams of being with him were nothing like the reality.

In my dreams, not only was he perfect, but I was as well.

Reality, not so much.

After another scorching round of mind-bending sex, Mikhail laid on his back and threw an arm over his eyes. His heavy breathing slowed. I did not know if he had fallen asleep or not. It would be understandable. The man had been up for two days straight, overseeing the security of Gregor and Samara's wedding and then rushing in to save me.

I tried to close my eyes as well. The moment I did, crushing doubt and insecurities crowded my already overwhelmed and exhausted mind.

This was too much — way too much.

This wasn't me. I wasn't *this* girl. Girls like me didn't get men like Mikhail. The man was like a dark, super-kinky James Bond. He probably dated women who wore expensive perfume, spoke French, walked around in lingerie and played Baccarat in exclusive Monaco casinos. Sophisticated women who liked champagne and caviar. Women who actually knew how to play sex games and didn't cry at the idea of trying to deep throat a sex toy.

I wasn't one of those women.

I thought I was.

I wanted to be one of them for him, and for me.

But I'd lied.

I'd lied when I said I could take all his brutal sexuality.

I was in way, way over my head with him.

The dream of wanting to be with Mikhail and the harsh reality of actually finally being with him collided in my head and body. And all I kept thinking was, I was a fraud. This wasn't me.

I wore Doc Martens and babydoll dresses. More often than not I smelled like oxyfuel from my jewelry welding torch, not perfume. The only set of matching lingerie I had ever owned was given to me by Yelena years ago when she stole it from Victoria's Secret as a gift for my seventeenth birthday. I had never even taken it out of the tissue-paper and ribbon wrapping. The only card game I knew was Texas Hold'em, and I hated champagne. My idea of a perfect date was a pizza and binge-watching something on Netflix while cuddling on my sofa.

This was all wrong.

I opened my eyes, and I gazed around his bedroom.

Look at his place. This must be what Batman's bedroom looks like. It was all sleek and new — and very grey — the walls, the bed covering, the electronics. Lots of grey. And who had windows like this in their bedroom? I mean I knew we were higher than most buildings, but still!

I thought of my cozy little apartment over my jewelry shop. Refusing any additional money from my brothers beyond what they were spending to help me set up my business, I had spent countless weekends going to flea markets, garage sales, and thrift shops to find all the eclectic pieces that cluttered the shelves and tables. None of the furniture matched, and I liked it that way. I guess it felt like the home I never had growing up.

My childhood home had been a fortress. Since it was more of a showpiece for my father's business and my mother's social ambitions, it was never much of a home. We could never leave toys lying around or even put our artwork on the fridge. My brothers were several years older than me and my parents couldn't be bothered, so I spent many countless hours playing alone in my bedroom. And even that wasn't much of a sanctuary. My mom had it decorated like she wanted, so they never allowed me to put my own toys on the shelves or posters of boy bands on the walls.

I didn't have any happy memories of my own, so I filled my new apartment with the discarded memories of others. Old photos of great-grandparents that I liked to pretend were mine. Cookie and biscuit tins from the fifties, which covered the tops of my kitchen cabinets. Slightly yellow lace doilies on every surface. And color… lots and lots of color. I also loved fresh flowers. I never went to the grocery store without buying a fresh bunch each week. I guess after working with cold metal all day, it was nice to climb the stairs to my warm little apartment and see color and a little bit of nature.

I looked at the alarm clock by his bedside. It was already early morning. Gregor and Damien would expect an update from Mikhail. They would want answers about last night. They weren't alone. I did as well, and this time I would not let them put me off. This time, they were going to tell me all about the family business, every detail. I had earned a right to know.

Carefully, I moved one leg out from under the covers and put it on the floor. I then shimmied my hips to the edge. Thank God Mikhail wasn't the cuddling type. He was lying on the other side of the enormous bed with his arm still over his eyes. I had to suppress a giggle at the thought of a man like Mikhail wanting to spoon with me after sex.

Especially the uncontrolled, taboo sex we'd just had.

Holy shit, that was intense.

It was a helluva way to finally lose my annoying virginity and certainly beat the pop culture version of some awkward fumbling in the back of some boy's used car.

I mean, it's no great surprise. After that kinky spanking he had given me a few years ago, I knew then he liked it rough. But hell, I don't think some of what we just did was even *legal* in some states.

The spanking.
The dirty talk.
The sex toys.

It was all straight out of a sexy movie. Although I had always fantasized about such things, I never thought people actually did them in *actual life*.

I placed my other foot on the floor and slowly raised my shoulders up. I had just pushed the covers off my hips when I was snatched backwards. Before I could blink, I was flat on my back with a large angry male straddling me. Mikhail grabbed my wrists and forced my arms over my head.

"Where do you think you're going?"

So I guess that answered my question as to if he was asleep or not. I should have known better than to think a former soldier like Mikhail would just blissfully fall asleep next to me as if he didn't have a care in the world. He probably usually slept with his eyes open, standing up, and only for a few minutes at a time.

It was too crass and beneath both of us for me to say 'you got what you wanted.'

"I... I... thought we were done?"

His sapphire blue eyes appeared black in the darkening light.

"Done?"

I could feel his cock harden as it pressed against my stomach.

"Does that feel like we're done?" he growled as his head lowered. He scraped the edge of his teeth along the column of my neck, soothing the sting with small licks. I raised my hips to grind against his own.

"That's it, babygirl. Let me in. I promise I'll make the pain worth it."

I was already embarrassingly wet as he forced his thick length into my still sore pussy.

God help me, I liked the pain, and he totally made it worth it.

An hour later, I was lying on my side, with Mikhail holding me from behind. Spooning me. *Who knew?* Could I be wrong about him?

"Mikhail. I know you don't want to hear this, but I really have to go. My brothers are going to be extremely worried about me."

Mikhail gave me a kiss on the shoulder before rising out of the bed. "You're right. Besides, the sooner I tell them about us the better."

"Us?"

"Yes, us."

I twisted the sheet between my fingers. "I don't think there's any reason to rush telling my brothers." Nothing had changed in three years. There was no way they would be okay with me being with Mikhail. They had made it clear it was a non-starter with them, although they had never given me a solid reason.

Mikhail crossed around the bed to my side. Standing before me, he used his finger to lift my gaze. It wasn't necessary. There was no way I was going to stare straight ahead. With my short stature and his height, his slowly hardening cock was right at my mouth. My cheeks flamed.

"Baby, what do I have to do to make you understand?"

"Understand what?"

"You're mine. There is no going back. It's a done deal.

You're not leaving my side, which means your brothers need to know."

"You act like you lov — you act like you like me or something," I stammered. I was acting like a lame schoolgirl again. Blushing over a boy. Afraid to even use the word love.

Mikhail smoothed the curls away from my face. "My adorable kroshka. We're well past *like*."

"I'm not like the women you are used to. I'm painfully shy and despite my upbringing, I'm really not the least bit sophisticated. I hate classical music and lobster. I can't stand getting dressed up for parties. I enjoy staying in to watch movies and eating pizza and going to flea markets. I can't speak French, bras are annoying, and I don't even know how to play Baccarat!"

Mikhail laughed. It stunned me. He looked like a different person when he laughed. The corners of his eyes crinkled as his gorgeous mouth broke into a wide smile. I was so used to seeing his lips thin in a stern line as he kept his emotions and features in check, it was a startling transformation.

"I don't have the first idea how to play Baccarat either, and I fully support your position if you want to give up wearing bras."

"But…."

Mikhail placed his hands on my shoulders and pulled me upright. Cupping the back of my head, he pressed me against his chest as he held me close. With our bodies still warm from the bed, it was incredibly comforting. I just wanted to sink into the strength and promise of his arms.

"I think one of the most adorable things about you is

that you have absolutely no idea how incredibly sexy and intriguing you are to me."

I tried to pull back from his embrace to look at his face, but he held me firm.

"Me? Seriously?"

It was still too hard for me to believe.

There had to be a catch.

Another shoe was about to drop.

"Now is not the time to discuss this. We have to get you back to Gregor's where I can keep you safe. Then we will handle the issue of us with your brothers. Now go in and take a shower. We have to leave in a half hour," he commanded with a light smack to my ass.

The entire time in the shower, I spun the crazy series of the events of this day over in my head. From the men who tried to kill me, to learning about my brother's surveillance of my life, to Mikhail and me finally having sex. It was a complete tangled mess. More than ever, I couldn't wait to ask Samara and Yelena for their advice. They would know what to do, I was sure of it. They definitely wouldn't let a man just sweep in and take control of their lives like I was doing with Mikhail right now. The problem was, I didn't see any way out of it. The bigger problem was, I wasn't sure I wanted one.

I never really wanted to be with a guy who was crazy wealthy, like my family. I craved normalcy. I wanted to be with an average guy who enjoyed going to the movies and taking advantage of GrubHub restaurant coupons. I guess I always assumed Mikhail made a modest salary, which had always appealed to me. It's not like I wasn't accustomed to big houses and wealth. I just was never comfortable with it.

There was no denying that the money to live in a place like this probably didn't come legally. When I learned about the more unsavory aspects of my family's so-called import-export business, I guess I pushed to the back of my mind what those details meant about Mikhail and his position within the family business. It was so naïve of me to think that security for my brothers was just Mikhail's day job and that he had nothing to do with their criminal lifestyle.

I gave myself a mental shake. I had enough on my plate dealing with whoever had just tried to kill me and this dramatic change to my relationship with Mikhail without worrying too far into the future. After all, having sex changed nothing. I wasn't sure if I was going to forgive him for all the surveillance and high-handed interference in my life. We may not have a future.

There was a bag filled with new clothes resting on the bed when I got out of the shower.

Mikhail walked into the bedroom. His hair was wet, and he was dressed in black fatigues with a long-sleeve black thermal shirt. There must have been a second bedroom somewhere. Of course, there must have been. This place was probably one of those penthouses that took up half the building floor. It stood in stark contrast to my little thousand square foot one-bedroom apartment.

"Are these for me?"

Mikhail nodded. "It's amazing what you can get delivered nowadays. I need you to be wearing something more *appropriate* than a babydoll dress on the off chance we run into more trouble."

I looked into the bag, then back at him. Adjusting my towel, I shyly averted my gaze.

Mikhail chuckled. "I'll give you some privacy to change."

I let out the breath I had been holding. It was silly, really, given what we had just done in his bed, twice, three times if you count the time he — no, I couldn't start thinking about all that again.

Reaching into the bag, I pulled out a pair of black cargo pants and a black turtleneck. Feeling rather naughty, I put them both on without putting my panties and bra back on. They fit perfectly. I walked back into the bathroom and caught sight of myself in the mirror.

I kind of looked like a badass.

I had never dressed all in black before. I always thought Samara and Yelena looked so fierce when they did so. Like they could tackle anything that came their way. Too bad I didn't really wear makeup. For the first time, I was a little curious what I would look like with bright red lipstick on. I fluffed my still damp curls and continued to stare at my reflection. I couldn't find a hair dryer, which meant my hair was going to dry in a riot of wavy, strawberry blonde curls. Usually I would tame it up in a messy bun, but I was glad I didn't have a scrunchie on me. I liked the idea of my hair appearing wild and teased out. It fit with my outfit, giving me an odd surge of confidence.

Maybe this wasn't so much about Mikhail and what he liked.

Could it be he was seeing something in me I was only just now recognizing?

It was funny. When we first met, Yelena informed me my zodiac sign was a Leo and that according to my sign, I was supposed to be dramatic and bold.

It always bugged her I was the exact opposite.

She used to tell me to embrace my inner lion.

I told her the signs were wrong.

She would always say the signs were never wrong.

Maybe she was right.

I couldn't wait to see Yelena and tell her.

Roar!

CHAPTER 17

Nadia

Mikhail was at the dining room table preparing his equipment when I emerged from the bedroom. The familiar scent of gun oil filled the room as he reassembled a gun.

I looked down at the weapon. "Is that a Mossberg 500?"

Mikhail hesitated. "Yes," he finally answered.

In a lame attempt at a distraction and to relieve the tension in the room, I picked up the box of ammunition he had on the table. "Brenneke Maximum Barrier Penetrating 12-gauge shotgun slugs," I said as I read the package. My laugh had a high-pitched, tinny quality which showed my nervousness, as I joked, "Are you planning on shooting through a cement wall?"

"A brick one, actually."

"Seriously?"

Mikhail nodded. "I suspect it may have been some hired hacks of the Novikoffs who attacked you. If I'm right, his sons hold late night events in their father's house when he is out of town. According to my intel, they sit with their backs to the wall and drink their father's vodka and smoke his expensive cigars. If we need to send a message to them and their father, I want to be prepared."

I was oddly pleased he had shared that information with me. I was half-expecting him to just brush me off. "Are you going to use a Range-R?"

Mikhail put down the gun he was holding and turned his full attention to me. "Of course."

A Range-R was a sophisticated motion detector which could read the slightest movement through any kind of wall. If a guy was breathing inside a closet deep inside of a house, the Range-R would pick it up. Unlike in the movies, heat sensing detectors did not work through walls.

I continued, "You'll have to get within a hundred yards."

Mikhail's brow furrowed as he continued to scrutinize me. He answered carefully, "That's the plan."

I shook my head. "This is the wrong ammunition. Do you have any of the Special Forces Short Magnums?"

Mikhail sat back in his chair. He tossed an arm over the back and stared up at me, a bemused smile on his face. "What is happening here?"

I flipped my hair over my shoulder and smoothed down my black turtleneck, embracing my new badass persona. Tilting my chin in the air, I asked, "Why? Are you impressed?"

He nodded. "Yes… and a little confused."

It wasn't a big mystery. When I was a little girl, virtually the only time I got to spend with my much older brothers was when they sat around the kitchen table cleaning their guns. They often talked about velocity, caliber, trajectory, barrel rifling, and the like. I would sit there and listen as I watched them take each gun apart, clean it, and reassemble it. Sometimes they would even let me polish the rifle barrels. Of course, I was naïve enough to believe it when they said they were using the guns for hunting and target shooting. I didn't realize they meant of human beings.

I shrugged. "I learned from my brothers."

Mikhail flipped one of the shotgun slugs between his fingers as he considered what I said. After a moment's pause, he responded, "You're wrong. These have thirty-five hundred feet of pounds energy with a sixteen hundred-fifty velocity straight out of the muzzle."

"Exactly. It will punch an immense hole in the wall but will lose much of its forward momentum doing it. The Special Forces short magnums are slightly less with only a fourteen hundred-seventy-six velocity out of the muzzle but will create a smaller hole allowing for a more precise hit."

Mikhail's eyebrows shot up. "Actually, you're right. I'll switch to the short magnums."

I felt a surge of pride.

Mikhail moved to stand before me. He cupped my jaw and bent down to nibble at my lower lip. "Do you have any idea how fucking sexy you are right now? If we had the time, I would toss you up on this table, spread your legs, and make a meal of you."

Oh. My. God.

It was too much. After growing accustomed to his cold and distant intensity over the years, I couldn't deal with this new, aggressively possessive Mikhail. Nervously laughing, I stepped back, breaking his embrace. "Too bad there are a bunch of homicidal idiots after me, and possibly my family, right now."

He shrugged as if I had just said too bad the sun wasn't shining. His casual demeanor toward the threat against my family could only mean it wasn't an unusual occurrence. It was a chilling thought.

He rubbed the back of his knuckles down my cheek. "The moment I put a bullet in each of their heads, I'm carrying you back to my bed and not letting you leave it for a week."

How romantic, just what every girl dreams of hearing her boyfriend say.

In all the times I'd imagined Mikhail and I finally getting together, it was never like this. Never over a table of guns, casually chatting about murder. I envisioned slightly awkward dinners with my brothers, with them teasing Mikhail about dating their little sister, and lazy Saturday mornings strolling around the Eastern Market sipping coffees. It really was jarring how deliberately obtuse I had been over the years about both my brothers and Mikhail. The signs were all there. I just hadn't wanted to see them.

After last night, I had no choice but to accept that I

was not just the little sister of the Ivanov brothers. I was a member of the powerful Ivanov mafia family. And apparently now the girlfriend of one of their top enforcers. The problem was, I wasn't sure I wanted to be. How could I have gotten this so wrong? It's like all this time I'd been thinking of Mikhail like he was Kevin Costner from *The Bodyguard*, all silent and strong and brooding but secretly sweet and protective. Now I'm wondering if he's more like Mark Wahlberg from *Fear*, all intense and possessive and maybe a tiny bit homicidal.

Maybe I wasn't being fair to him. It had been a rather extreme twelve hours between the wedding, the break-in at my shop, him murdering three people, us finally having sex. Technically, not just sex, more like mind-blowing, completely twisted, crazy orgasmic, spank-me-again, pound the sheets sex. Maybe I needed to wait till things calmed down? Maybe he was just in some kind of high alert, extreme soldier mode after the attack, and he'll go back to being the strong, silent, sweetly protective Mikhail I had built up in my imagination.

Not knowing what to do with my hands, I fidgeted with the sniper scope on an M16A4. "Can we swing by my shop on the way to Gregor's? I need to grab a few things."

Mikhail stroked my hair, then gave the back of my neck a quick squeeze. "Sorry, baby, no. You can't go back there."

"But I need my purse, my cellphone, clothes to wear. How long till I can go back?"

"When I say you can't go back, I mean, ever. They have compromised the space."

"Ever? I didn't agree to that. I told you I had no intention of moving or closing my store."

"You realize there are three dead bodies lying in there right now?"

"So? We can get rid of the bodies and just clean up the blood."

Get rid of the bodies and clean up the blood? Who am I?

Did I really just say that? How horrifying to think how easy it was to fall prey to this whole mafia family mentality. If this was how I was after only a few hours of coming to terms with the true, brutal reality of what my brothers, and Mikhail, did to earn money, what would I be like a year from now? Two years? Ten? A lifetime? A cartoonish image of me sporting a thick New York accent drinking red wine as I chatted with Yelena and Samara about a new laundry solution I had found to get the blood out of Mikhail's dress shirts flashed across my mind. And what if we had kids? Would our children follow in their daddy's footsteps?

Shaking my head, I tried to focus on the super tall, angry man in front of me. "I made it clear I would not allow last night's events to derail my career or my life."

"And I told you it wasn't negotiable. You're done there. My men will pack up whatever you need from your apartment. I'll make sure of it, after I've taken care of… things."

I crossed my arms over my chest. "I don't want you or your men going through my stuff. Why can't I just go with you and pack while you are taking care of *things*?"

Things like murder, mayhem, and dead body disposal.
Just boyfriend things.

He angrily started to shove his guns into a large black

duffel bag. "For starters, because you are still in danger, and I'm not letting you go back there. That's why. And secondly, because I said so."

My mouth dropped open as I raised my arms, palms out. "You seriously didn't just say *because I said so*, as if I were some child to be ordered about?"

Mikhail took my chin in his hand. "Act like a child, get treated like one. Maybe I need to flip you over my knee and remind you who's in charge now?"

I tightened my inner thighs. It was so taboo, so wrong, but damn if the idea didn't make my stomach flip. How was this even possible? I was beyond pissed at him. I was still sore from the intense fucking he had just given me. Never mind the fact that it was also my first time, although the furthest thing I was feeling right now was virginal.

What kind of dark magic hold did he have over me that I could feel myself get warm at just the idea of his hand on my ass? A sick, twisted part of me wanted to push him further. A vision of hot, angry sex with Mikhail sprang up in my mind. The kind of sex that would make me scream with pleasure and pain as I cried for mercy but received none. My chest tightened as my cheeks flushed. It was hard to breathe as I imagined those strong tattooed arms holding me down as I fought and clawed to be set free. If I made him mad enough, would he follow through with his threat to take my ass, my ultimate taboo fantasy? The thought terrified and thrilled me.

Did I dare?

Taking a deep breath, I said the one thing I knew would completely set him off. "Poshel na khuy, Mikhail!"

Time stopped.

His hands closed into fists at his sides as his eyes narrowed. Slowly, as if a massive, terrifying mountain had suddenly come to life, he took two measured steps toward me.

My heart stopped. Fuck. This was a mistake. Oh my God! What had I done?

I held up a placating hand. "Wait, I—"

Before I could even finish my sentence, he lunged.

CHAPTER 18

Mikhail

I CARRIED her struggling over my shoulder into the bedroom, where I threw her down onto the center of the bed, before meaningfully returning to lock the door.

"We don't have time for this, Mikhail! You said my brothers were waiting for us."

"They'll wait," I said as I unbuckled my belt.

"Look, I shouldn't have said that. I was just trying to make you mad."

"You succeeded."

"You can't be serious about this?"

"Does it look like I'm serious?"

Nadia scrambled over to the other side of the bed and hopped off. "Look. I'm sorry! Okay! I shouldn't have said it. It was beyond stupid, and I regretted it the moment I did it."

"While that's nice to hear, it will not change your punishment."

"Punishment?"

"You heard me."

"This is insane!"

Stripping off my belt, I folded the thick leather between my hands as I approached her.

"You know what's insane? You refusing to obey me when I only have your safety in mind."

Nadia's cute mouth opened in protest, and then quickly shut.

"I realize things are really fucked up right now. Baby, I understand more than you know. But that does not give you the right to run around acting like a petulant brat putting yourself in danger."

I truly understood. A person didn't live my kind of life and not experience tragedy. I knew the grief and anxiety she must have been feeling over what happened last night. The problem was these very things seemed to make her reckless. I'd seen it happen before. The idea that life was uncertain, so why give a damn. Whether or not she recognized it herself, I knew her well enough to know this careless attitude toward her safety was going to get her killed. And that was unacceptable.

My babygirl was too important to me, especially now that I had finally decided to claim her as my own. I hadn't gone to extreme lengths to keep her safe from a distance only to lose her when she was directly under my protection. Fuck no. What she needed was an extreme release. Someone to exorcise her demons. There was nothing like a good hard fuck to calm the soul.

I watched as she paced on the other side of the bed. Her wild curls floated over her shoulders and down her back. Soon those same curls would be wrapped around my fist. She gestured wildly as she tried to talk her way out of the punishment we both knew she secretly craved. Secretly needed.

"You put security cameras—"

Nice try.

She would not make me feel guilty over keeping her safe.

"Yes. I've been watching over you. Yes. I know that was wrong, but kroshka, I did it for the right reasons, and I will show you every one of those reasons every fucking day for the rest of our lives as soon as you are safe."

I could see her resolve melting. Her beautiful eyes were darkening to a deep bluish grey like the sky before a storm. Careful not to arouse her suspicion, I moved a few steps closer, treating her like a wild animal that needed taming. I now had her cornered between the bed and the far bedroom wall. Her only escape was through me.

"But right now, you and I are going to get a few things straight before we leave this room."

"I said I was sorry. I admit it was stupid to try and insist on going back to my apartment right now."

"Yes, it was. You can't keep fighting me, baby. It's too dangerous. When I say I need your complete obedience, no questions asked, I fucking mean it."

I watched as she nervously fiddled with the hem of her shirt, keeping her head down, refusing to meet my gaze.

After a long moment, she whispered, "Sorry."

Hearing her submissively apologize to me sent a frisson of raw lust straight to my cock.

It was time to show her just how sorry she was going to be.

"On your knees," I growled.

"Please. I'm scared. I know you're angry…."

"You should be scared, kroshka. Teper' vstan' na koleni."

Still, Nadia hesitated. Without warning, I whipped the belt around her neck and used it to yank her to me. Bending down, I met her upturned face. Our lips were only a breath apart. "I said get on your knees."

Releasing the beast inside of me, I dropped the belt, fisted her hair and pushed her onto her knees.

Keeping my grip on her hair, I slowly unzipped my jeans. Her lower lip quivered. I knew she was remembering earlier when I made her swallow that silicone dick.

Remembering how she struggled to accept its length down her throat.

Remembering my warning that my cock was longer and thicker.

I pulled my shaft free. Gripping it, I ran my hand up and down its length. Nadia tried to pull back, but I refused to loosen my grip on her hair.

"Open your mouth."

Nadia cried, "Please. I can't do this."

"You'll do as I tell you. Now open your mouth."

Her pink lips barely opened. I didn't care. It would just give the added pleasure of forcing my cock in. Edging closer, I placed one foot on either side of her knees. I wanted her to feel caged in. As if she had no choice, because she didn't. I placed the head of my fisted cock against her lower lip. I could feel her gasping exhale over the sensitive tip moments before I pushed in. The first thing I felt was the slight scrape of her bottom teeth. The hint of pain barely tempered my response. I pushed in further. Her tongue moved along the bottom ridge of my cock as she tried to adjust to the feeling of having my hard flesh fill her mouth.

Her small hands rose to press against my thighs. I could tell her to lower them, but I liked the idea of her trying in vain to push back. I had the leveraged position. There was nothing she could do to prevent me from fucking her mouth.

With that thought, I thrust.

Nadia gagged. Her mouth closed. I could feel the press of her teeth. I jerked on her hair, pulling her head back. I thrust again. This time I could actually feel her startled scream as my cock pressed against the back of her throat. Her nails dug into my thighs. I refused to relent.

Pulling back slightly, to allow her one gasping breath, I warned, "You're going to swallow every inch, babygirl."

Using both hands to hold her head steady, I forced my cock past her lips again. I watched as her lips stretched thin over the thickening base of my cock as I pushed in deeper. She had only taken about half. I had yet to push into her throat.

The room filled with the sounds of my own heavy breathing and her whimpering. I pulsed my hips back and forth, gently pressing at the back of her throat, exhausting her gag reflex. When she was ready, I thrust forward. Pushing past her resistance, I could feel the tight grip of her throat as my shaft slid in deep. With my grip on her head, I tilted her head back to create a smooth column. I gave one last thrust. Her chin brushed against my balls. I stayed buried deep inside her throat for a moment before I relented and pulled free. Nadia collapsed forward, her head resting against my hip as she coughed and desperately tried to suck in gasps of air. I pulled on her hair to move her back into position.

"Open wide for me."

Nadia obeyed.

This time, I didn't hesitate. I drove my cock straight down her throat, feeling her gag reflex tighten around my shaft as I moved in and out. My balls tightened. I had to pull free. I wasn't ready to come just yet.

I still had plans for her.

Lifting her up by her hair, I tossed her facedown onto the bed. Before she could cry out, I had wrenched her cargo pants down to her knees. Her pale bottom was on full display. I had a flash of regret that there was no mark on her flesh from my earlier punishments. I wanted to see my brand on her. A hint of a bruise. The barest outline of a handprint in a bright red to match that cute heart tattoo of hers. Something to claim her as my own. I would have to remedy that situation soon.

I watched her clutch at the bedcovers as I spread her ass cheeks. Licking my thumb, I pressed it against her tight rosebud.

"No! No! Please! I promise I'll behave."

"I warned you, baby. Time to accept your punishment."

I palmed her pussy. Pressing my two middle fingers between her folds, I felt her slick arousal. She could cry and protest all she wanted, but we both knew she liked my rough handling. She liked my punishments. There was something intoxicating about corrupting the innocent. My little Nadia was so sweet and naïve, despite her dangerous family.

It was a marvel, really. Some of the most dangerous people in the world had surrounded her her entire life, and yet she'd maintained her fresh sweet innocence until now. Still, from the moment I'd met her I sensed there was something more, something hidden deep. So deep perhaps she wasn't even aware of it. The desire to *feel* something. Really feel it. Down to the bone. Life had a way of making a person numb, forcing them to hide the pain behind a sweet facade. Eventually, they stopped feeling altogether. I knew I wanted to be the man to make her feel.

"Tilt up on your toes," I commanded, my voice gravelly with barely leashed desire.

The moment her hips shifted, I pierced her with my two fingers, knowing it would cause an initial sharp pain deep inside her tight pussy. Nadia groaned in response and ground her hips against the edge of the bed.

I pushed my fingers in and out of her tight little body, violently fucking her with my hand. Nadia screamed as her hips bounced up and down. I added a third finger. Her body clenched. Relentlessly, I shoved them into her cunt, forcing her body to accept them. Nadia writhed under my rough touch. Unable to resist the lure of her pale skin any longer, I slapped her ass with my free hand and relished the sight of my red handprint on her cheek. I spanked her again and again. Nadia screamed in response. Her release gripped my fingers. I loved how wet my baby got from my touch.

After thrusting my fingers inside her a few more times, I slowly withdrew them and traced a path to her asshole. Her flesh glistened as I circled her quivering entrance with her own wet heat. Unable to wait another moment, I stepped close. Nadia was still lost in the power of her own release, so she didn't react at first. Then she felt the press of my cock. She jolted upright. Placing my hand between her shoulder blades, I forced her back down.

"You can't. You're too big," she whined.

I ignored her pleas. Gripping my shaft, I pressed the head against her puckered entrance, watching as it compelled her unwilling body to submit.

"Ow! Ow! It hurts!"

The pale pink skin whitened as I thrust forward. The head of my cock disappeared into her body. Her delicate ring of muscle then closed around the slightly thinner shaft. My cock was still wet from her mouth as I shifted my hips forward. I had to hold her hips down as Nadia wriggled and moaned. Shifting my hands, I placed one on each cheek and stretched her open wide, adding to her humiliation. She was bared and vulnerable to me. I moved slowly, giving her body a limited amount of time to adjust to the painful intrusion of my cock, knowing that once I was fully seated in her ass, I would thrust, and once I started, I wouldn't stop, no matter how loud she screamed.

I knew a full nine inches was a lot to expect of her, especially knowing she was an anal virgin, but I didn't

BETRAYED HONOR

care. It would never get easier, so she might as well learn to accept my full length from the very beginning, since I planned to fuck her tight ass every chance I got.

Watching her body submit and accept my cock sent a surge of possessive fire deep into my gut. I was never letting this woman go. Ever.

As soon as my balls brushed the underside of her ass cheeks, I stopped.

"Where is my cock?"

The bed covers and her own tears muffled her response.

I spanked her other ass cheek.

"Where is my cock?"

"In my ass."

"Why?"

"Because I was a bad girl," she whimpered. "I promise I'll be good. Please, just take it out. Please!"

"No, baby. You want to please me, don't you?"

She sniffed. "Yes," she whimpered.

"Well, I want to fuck your ass till you scream."

Nadia sobbed. "I'm scared. It hurts too much. Please, I can't."

Knowing she needed to feel more of a connection with me, I carefully pulled out. Her sigh of relief would be short-lived.

Taking her hips, I flipped her over onto her back and lifted her legs high, till they rested over my shoulders. Her eyes were bright with tears as they streamed down her flushed cheeks. She looked beautiful.

I slipped my cock between her pussy folds, brushing her still sensitive clit as I wet my shaft. Then taking hold of her knees, I spread her legs wide and stepped closer. She knew my intentions the moment she felt the press of my cock at her now sore asshole.

"No! I thought you were done!" Her hands reached down to cover her pussy and try to block my cock.

"Not even close, kroshka. Now move your hands before I tie you up."

Reluctantly, her arms fell uselessly to her sides. Her tiny hole was now slightly slack. I easily popped the head in. Her fists gripped the covers.

"Hold on, baby. Now is when the real pain starts."

I thrust deep.

Nadia's head tilted back as she let loose a deep-throated howl.

I thrust again. Soon I was lost in the ecstasy of her body as I forced it to give me pleasure through her pain.

Releasing her legs, I leaned over her as I thrust. I shoved her turtleneck up high, till her breasts were exposed, then flicked her nipple with my tongue. I sucked it in deep, gently using my teeth to bite the delicate flesh before moving to her other nipple.

"Oh God! It hurts! Please come! Please come!" she begged as her head thrashed from side to side.

Reaching between our joined bodies, I dipped my fingers into her cunt. I could feel the press of my cock through the thin wall between her cunt and ass. I stretched my arm over her body.

"Open your mouth," I commanded roughly.

She obeyed.

I pressed all three fingers into her mouth. "Suck them. Taste your own arousal. Taste how much you like the pain." As her tongue swept between my fingers, lapping up her own come, I continued to thrust in deep, punishing her with my cock. Her body tensed as her legs closed tighter around my hips, grinding her core against me. Her orgasm spurred my own.

My balls tightened as I pushed my fingers in deeper. Wanting to hear her gag and choke as if she were both sucking my cock as well as accepting it in her ass. Later, I would have to get her a dildo gag. The thought of her beautiful eyes looking up at me from over a black leather gag with a silicone cock forced deep into her throat brought my release roaring to the surface.

Throwing my head back, I groaned deeply and completely as I spilled my seed in her ass. My breathing heavy, I waited till my cock had slightly softened before pulling free. Nadia immediately tried to lower her legs and curl up.

"Don't," I ordered.

I grasped her ankles and stretched her legs up high. I wanted to take in the view of her abused asshole, now dark pink around her slack entrance. My thick come slowly dripped out.

Dipping my fingers between the folds of her cunt, I growled. "Let's see if I can make you come one more time."

Nadia's only response was a submissive moan.

CHAPTER 19

Mikhail

WE COULD HEAR the screams from outside on the doorstep.

Gregor opened the front door and ushered us inside. The screams and shouts got louder, except this time we could also hear pounding. I tilted my head to the side and listened. It was coming from upstairs.

Gregor gestured with his head. "We locked the girls in an upstairs bedroom till the entire premises was verified secure. They are… not happy about it."

He then gave Nadia and me the once-over. Raising an eyebrow, he asked, "Did you get lost?"

I deserved that. Under normal circumstances, after such a significant security breach, my ass would have raced straight here to secure the premises, instead of relying on my men to do so. I wasn't worried. Gregor and Damien were more than capable of protecting themselves and their women. The fact was these weren't normal circumstances. Everything changed the moment that black SUV drove up to Nadia's jewelry store, because I knew in my gut what was about to happen. Never again would I deny my feelings for her. From this point forward, she was mine and no one, not even her brothers, was going to take her away from me. As soon as we had this mess straightened out, I was going to have a conversation with Gregor and Damien telling them just that.

I loved them both as if they were truly my brothers, and I would always be grateful to them for taking a chance on me. It had been an honor working by their sides. My loyalty to them was as steadfast as it had always been. I just hoped they wouldn't see my love for their sister as a betrayal. They had warned me off and on over the years of how impossible a match was between us. And until yesterday, I had respected their decision, but no more.

Nadia would be my wife as soon as I could arrange it.

The Devil himself would not stop me, and neither would the Ivanov brothers.

My answer was evasive, for now. "I had to take care of a few things first."

Gregor's gaze shifted between me and Nadia. He wasn't a stupid man. In our business, instincts were always trusted, and I was certain by the set of his jaw and the narrowing of his eyes that he could sense something was different between Nadia and me.

Before he could say anything, Damien strolled into the

entryway from the kitchen. He jutted his chin out at me and repeated his brother's same question. "Get lost?"

Ignoring the jibe, I said, "I have an update."

Damien nodded. Then he crouched down and grabbed Nadia around the waist and hugged her close as he spun her around. Her blue eyes widened in surprise before she wrapped her arms around his neck and hugged him back. He placed her back on the ground and pulled her close, placing a kiss on the top of her head. "Never scare us like that again, okay, baby sis?"

Nadia's eyes teared up as she sniffed. She buried her head against his chest and nodded.

A sharp stab of jealousy pierced me. It was ludicrous. The man was her brother. Still, now that I had finally decided to claim her as my own, I found I didn't want anyone touching her or holding her close but me.

Gregor pulled her to his side and ruffled her already tangled curls. His next words belied his tender actions. "You ever disobey me like that again, and there will be consequences, you understand?"

My hand curled into a fist. The only thing worse than watching another man hug my girl was hearing one demanding her obedience. She would follow my rules from now on, not theirs. Something I would make very clear to them as soon as we'd handled today's business.

Setting Nadia aside, Gregor's gaze slipped to my fist. With an effort, I unlocked my fingers.

"Is Mother here?" asked Nadia. I could see the tension in her shoulders as she braced for the answer. Nadia's mother wasn't a bad person — just uninvolved in her children's lives.

Gregor rubbed his eyes. "No, thank God. She had a spa week in Arizona already planned so she could recover from all the wedding planning she *didn't* do. We sent a car over to her house and hustled her out early on the private plane."

All three siblings visibly relaxed. Myself, as well. If there was one thing their mother loved, it was gossip drummed up by drama. It was the last thing anyone needed right now.

The shouts and pounding, which had abated somewhat, started up again in earnest.

Nadia swiped at the tears on her cheeks with the back of her hand. "You don't really have Yelena and Samara locked in a bedroom?"

Gregor and Damien exchanged a look.

Her mouth fell open. "Are you both crazy?" Turning to Gregor, she said, "Samara is going to be mad as a wet hen at you," then turning to Damien, she warned, "and Yelena is going to shoot you dead."

Damien pulled something out of his pocket and opened his palm, displaying six .38 caliber bullets. "Already thought of that. I took the bullets out of her gun."

Nadia shook her head as she placed her fists on her hips. "You both are impossible. They're right, you're hopeless Neanderthal cavemen." She then tossed a meaningful glance over her shoulder at me.

I smiled back at her.

Guilty as charged.

Damien gestured to the upstairs. "How about you be a wonderful sister and run interference for me when I let them out?"

Nadia backed a step away as she waved her hands at him. "No way. You got yourself into this mess. You get yourself out."

Damien sighed. "Here I thought because you were dressed like a badass and all…." He let his words trail off.

We all watched for Nadia's reaction. Her shoulders swept back as she jutted out her chin. Smoothing the black turtleneck I'd given her over her abdomen, she asked, "You think I look like a badass?"

"It's a good look on you, baby sis."

Nadia relented. "Okay, I'll go with you, but if Yelena wants to knee you in the balls, I will not stand in her way."

Damien placed a hand over her shoulders and guided her to the staircase. "Agreed."

We all shared a look over her head.

He had no intention of letting the girls out. He was, however, going to lock Nadia in there with them.

As I watched them ascend the stairs, Gregor clapped me on the shoulder. "You look like you could use a drink."

It wasn't even noon, but then again, it was only vodka. "Hell yeah I could."

We both headed down the long narrow hallway to his study. As we crossed the threshold, Gregor angled off to the sideboard to pour us both a drink. My gaze strayed, as it always did when I was in this room, to his desk. I never saw ledger books and pens. I saw a smart-mouthed, strawberry blonde bent over it with her bare ass on display as she prettily confessed to being a bad girl as I spanked her.

I cleared my throat as I willed my hardened cock down. Accepting the glass from Gregor, I drained half the contents before speaking. "My men grabbed someone off the street I think is involved. They're waiting at the warehouse with him. I'm almost certain this is the work of the Novikoffs. We'll get confirmation soon."

Gregor crossed to the windows and looked out as he took a sip. He then turned to face me. "I agree. It has all the markings of their sloppy, half-assed way of doing things. They are also fans of hiring local idiots to do their dirty work. Still...."

I nodded. "I know what you're going to say. We had eyes and ears on Egor this whole time. If this was the Novikoffs, it wasn't sanctioned by him."

Gregor put his glass down. "I paid him off. I settled everything. You think his sons would be rash enough to start a new war without their father's permission?"

I shrugged. "You mean Dumb and Dumber? In a word, yes."

Egor's sons, Leonid and Lenin, shared the same half-brain. They were such stereotypically spoiled rich kids that they were a boring redundancy. If they weren't drunk, they were high. If they weren't balls deep in a whore, they were balls deep in some stupid mess of their own making. The only time they stopped shooting their mouths off about their family's confidential business is when they were passed out. I could definitely see those two bloated tick egos putting together a half-cocked plan to come after the Ivanovs.

Damien walked through the door. "It's done. Can't say you're going to have much of a honeymoon night after this, Gregor."

Now that all three were locked in the bedroom, I could only imagine what hellish retribution they were planning.

He winked. "It's okay. It's even more fun when she's mad at me."

I thought the same about Nadia, but since she was both men's little sister, I wisely kept my mouth shut.

"To the warehouse?" I asked as I picked up the black duffel bag I had dropped on the carpet.

Damien tossed over his shoulder as we all filed out, "I have a better idea. Call Ilya and tell him to bring the man to the jewelry store. Might as well kill two birds with one stone."

I agreed and pulled out my phone to contact Ilya, but something distracted my mind. I knew what we had planned for her jewelry store. It was too risky a possibility that a police detective not on our payroll would ferret out what had really happened and start asking unnecessary and dangerous questions. If I completely destroyed the crime scene, the evidence would tell a much murkier story. It would be filed away as a bungled burglary by some drug addicts who turned on one another. Case closed. So much of our power came from simply controlling the narrative. It was absolutely necessary, but at the same time, I knew it would devastate Nadia. I would just have to deal with the fallout later. My priority was keeping her safe, and to do that I had to send a clear message that going after my woman meant a slow and painful death to anyone involved.

We drove one of the older Range Rovers to her shop. Now that it was early afternoon, people would be around. There was no point in drawing attention to ourselves by rolling up in some flashy, luxury car. Just as I had last night, we parked in the alley and entered through the back door. Three bodies were stacked on the floor next to her workbench, but behind the counter, out of view of anyone who may have tried to peek past the curtains drawn across the storefront windows. Stacked in the center of the store were two red plastic gas cans and several tarps. The shelves that once glittered with silver jewelry on crystal and moss displays were gone. They had cleared everything out.

It was clear the cleaner crew had begun their work. Ilya and the rest of my men hadn't arrived yet from the warehouse.

Damien kicked at the stack of bodies till they rolled off of one another and lay sprawled face up on the floor. Neither he nor Gregor recognized the twitchy fucker I'd shot last. Gregor pulled the ski masks off the remaining two.

Damien kicked the boot of the man closest to him. "This asshole has definitely done work for Dumb and Dumber. Low-level shit. Shaking down corner dealers, that sort of thing."

Gregor took out his phone and took a close-up picture of each face as Ilya and two of my men burst through the back door dragging another man by the upper arms, a black hood over his head. They shoved him down by the shoulders to sit in the center of Nadia's secondhand sofa.

Ilya tossed me the key to our captive's handcuffs. "We have all of her things moved out of the apartment and all the jewelry stuff from here. A crew is bringing it to Gregor's."

I nodded. "Don't let any of the girls see them. Stash it all in one of the outer buildings."

Ilya said he'd make the call now, before leaving with the other men. They would wait outside for further instructions. We let no one see more than they absolutely needed to see.

I leaned over and uncuffed the man. The moment I did, he yanked off the hood and glared at us. Without saying a word, he shifted his bulky frame forward and spit on the ground at our feet.

Gregor raised an eyebrow. "Charming."

The man sneered. "Fuck you."

I gestured in his general direction. "Gentleman, this well-spoken man is Gary Glogowski, but he prefers his street moniker, Bruiser."

Damien let out a bark of laughter. "With a name like Gary Glogowski, so would I. Jesus Christ man, did your parents hate you even in the womb?"

The man shot to his feet. Bruiser was almost as tall as Damien, but unlike Damien, his bloated frame was more fat than muscle. "Fuck you."

I shot the toe of my heavy boot into his left kneecap, unbalancing Bruiser and sending him sprawling back onto the sofa. "Sit your ass down."

Gregor leaned down to retrieve the gun Twitchy used to threaten me, then rose. Without looking up, he slid the release back and chambered a bullet. He said with deadly calm, "Bruiser, I'm going to need you to marshal what few brain cells you may have, and try to string more than two words together, because I need answers."

Damien placed his right fist in his left palm and

cracked his knuckles. "Someone went after our little sister last night, and now someone has to pay."

Bruiser cocked his head to the side and rubbed the underside of his jaw with his knuckles. "You ladies are about to find out why they call me Bruiser."

I placed my palm over my heart. "Aw, baby's first sentence."

Damien wiped away a fake tear. "They grow up so fast."

Gregor rolled his eyes.

As Bruiser shot to his feet a second time, Gregor pointed the gun and fired.

Bruiser screamed and clutched his thigh before falling back. "I'll kill you for that. I'll kill your entire family. I'll kill everyone you—"

I waved my hand in the air. "Yeah, yeah, yeah. We got it. You'll kill everyone we love. We're really scared. Now start talking."

White foam formed at the corner of his thick lips as Bruiser sneered, "Fuck you."

I took the gun from Gregor. It was important we used the same one these assholes brought to the scene and not our own, so if there was an investigation, the crime scene would make sense and nothing would lead back to us. "I guess we're back to that."

Without saying another word, I fired a round into Bruiser's other thigh. He screamed in pain. He pressed his hands to the tops of both of his thighs, and thick blood pooled over his fingers to drench his pants and the faded daisy fabric on the sofa. Images of Nadia curled up sleeping on those same cushions made my stomach twist with bitter bile. It may upset her when she learned what we had done to her shop, but there was no fucking way I could ever let her come back. I could never tell her what happened here today. There was equally no chance in hell I would let her unknowingly, innocently curl up on that sofa again, no matter how clean the cleaning crew got it.

I sank down on my haunches, dangling the gun between my knees. "Here's the thing, Gary. May I call you Gary? I'm going to keep filling you with holes till you talk. Either way, you're dying today. It's just a matter of how painful you want your journey to hell to be."

Bruiser's fat lips puckered as he inhaled air through his nose. I lifted the gun again.

Bruiser blurted, "It was those two Russian idiots."

Gregor raised his phone and hit record. "You're going to have to be more specific, Gary. We know a lot of Russian idiots."

Bruiser grimaced as he clutched at his thighs. "Lenin and Leon Novakiss."

"Could you mean Lenin and Leonid Novikoff?" asked Damien.

Once Bruiser started talking, there was no shutting him up. "Yeah, those two. They asked me to arrange to kidnap the bitch, something stupid about family honor. We were supposed to take her to a crack house and juice her up good. The plan was to video her getting all kinds of nasty fucked by a bunch of guys for as long as it took her to die, then put it on the internet. I waited at the crack house"— Bruiser gestured with his head to the three bodies lying on the floor near the sofa— "but these fuckers never showed."

My entire body broke out in a cold sweat. Handing Gregor the gun, I took a few steps back, turned, and vomited the bile that had been roiling in my stomach. *Fuck.* Just the thought of that almost happening to my sweet babygirl made me sick with fear and disgust. Usually, I would have happily beat the man to death, but I didn't even want to touch him after hearing something so vile. Wiping my mouth with the back of my hand, I walked over to the gas cans and picked one up. I returned to where Bruiser sat bleeding and slowly unscrewed the cap.

His eyes widened. "You said if I talked, you'd kill me quickly."

I poured the gasoline over his head. Bruiser howled in agony as the noxious chemical hit his open bullet wounds.

I emptied the can over his body, and onto the sofa, then tossed it aside. "I said you had a choice on how painful your journey to hell would be. I said nothing about *my* choice on how painful it would be for you."

Damien poured gasoline around the shop while Gregor poured a straight path out the back door. Bruiser rolled off the sofa and landed with a thud on his stomach. Begging for mercy, he propped up on his forearms and tried to pull his considerable bulk toward the door, dragging his useless legs behind him.

Ignoring his pleas, we walked out the door. Opening the trunk of the Range Rover, I reached into my duffel bag and pulled out a plastic bottle of water and a t-shirt. I poured the water over all of our hands and wiped mine dry before tossing the shirt to Damien.

He held it up before wiping his hands. "A Nappoliano, nice choice."

I shrugged as I reached for the gold and black slim box of Sobranie cigarettes and lighter tucked into a side pocket. "You're not the only one who likes to look good."

Flipping open the box, I offered them each a cigarette. After holding up the lit flame for each of us to use, I tossed the lighter to Gregor. He turned and walked back to the building. When he opened the door, I could just make out Bruiser's form as he was still desperately dragging his body toward the exit.

Flicking the lid on the Zippo, Gregor tossed the open flame into the building and shut the door. I would have liked the honor myself, but as Nadia's eldest brother and head of the Ivanov family, by rights, it fell to him.

He returned and leaned against the car with Damien and me. We listened to Bruiser's agonized screams as black smoke crept through the narrow gap around the door.

I took a final drag off my cigarette and tossed it into the alley dirt. "Gentlemen, time to go hunting."

CHAPTER 20

Nadia

I STARED at the closed door.

Damien had locked me in and, what's worse, I'm pretty sure Mikhail knew he was going to do it. The moment he opened the door, there was a shove between my shoulder blades. I fell into Yelena's arms. Before either of us could react, the door slammed shut, and we heard the ominous click of the lock sliding into place.

Samara, who was sitting on the bed dressed in her usual outfit of a paint-splattered t-shirt, wide-cuffed dark jeans, and a lipstick red bandana around her hair, popped the top of a McDonald's hash brown into her mouth and said, "Welcome home, Sis!"

Yelena flopped down on the bed beside her before reaching for a large styrofoam cup, which I was certain contained a Cafe Mocha, knowing them both. "For at least an hour, they lured us in here with the promise of a McDonald's Egg McMuffin."

Pulling one of the small, upholstered bucket chairs closer to the bed, I sat down and peeked inside the slightly crumpled brown to-go bag. Inside was a third uneaten McMuffin. "That rat bastard," I marveled as I reached for the yellow-wrapped breakfast sandwich. Mikhail knew what my brothers had planned before even taking me here. That's why he'd said we would get breakfast at Gregor's when I said we should swing through a drive-through on our way.

Yelena leaned back and plucked a third Cafe Mocha from the cup holder on the nightstand. "It's cold but still drinkable."

I shook my head as I took it. "He knew they were going to lock me in here, too."

Samara picked at her hash brown, popping another piece in her mouth. "We were going to warn you, but the cavemen took our phones," she said using their collective, and rather fitting, nickname for Gregor and Damien.

I shrugged. "Wouldn't have helped. My phone's dead and still plugged in back at the store."

Yelena and Samara exchanged a worried look.

Yelena played with the plastic tab on her mocha cup. "Do you want to talk about what happened?"

I thought they would never ask. I wanted to be sympathetic to them being locked in a bedroom because of me all morning, but I was dying to tell them about Mikhail and everything that happened this morning. I desperately needed their advice.

Nodding, I said, "God, yes."

They both squealed and moved closer to the edge of the bed as they sat up straighter.

Before I could begin, Yelena gestured to my outfit. "Loving the Tomb Raider chic thing you have going on here. I never thought you'd give up those babydoll dresses of yours. Although, I see you still have the pink Doc Martens, but with this outfit they work."

I adjusted the collar on my turtleneck. "Thank you. Mikhail got it for me."

Samara leaned in. "And exactly *why* did you need new clothes?"

Yelena snatched the corner piece of orange cheese from the Egg McMuffin in my hand. "Tell us everything."

"Okay, but you have to promise not to tell my brothers. They'd lose it."

Yelena drew her thumb and forefinger across her lips. "Our lips are sealed. Now spill it."

I started with how Mikhail kissed me behind the cathedral right after the wedding.

Samara's mouth fell open. "Just like that, after all these years, he finally kissed you?"

I nervously twisted my fingers. "Not exactly. There's something I never had time to tell you both."

I then backtracked and told them about the night of my eighteenth birthday party.

Yelena cried out. Grabbing one of the bed pillows, she tossed it at my head. "How come you didn't tell us?"

I hugged the pillow to my stomach. "It was right before you both ran away. What was I supposed to say?" Looking straight at Samara, I continued, "Sorry my big, super scary older brother is forcing you to marry him, but let me tell you about how Mikhail spanked me and called me his dirty girl?"

"Yes!" they both shouted in unison.

Yelena shook her head. "So for all these years he hasn't touched you or made a pass or *anything* until yesterday?"

I popped the lid off my mocha and swirled around the last few swallows to capture all the chocolate syrup. "Nope. It was like he barely knew I was alive."

Samara chuckled. "I have a feeling he knows you're alive now."

Since both of them had shared all the kinky details of their relationships with my brothers, despite my countless protests of 'Ew that's my brother you're talking about,' I knew I didn't have to hold anything back with them.

It was difficult telling them about the part where I was attacked. For starters, I completely wanted to forget about it. That wasn't the healthiest. Countless magazine articles and Oprah shows would tell me to deal with my trauma and feelings, but it was my choice not to. It would open up a Pandora's box. Once I went down that path, it wouldn't just be about the attack. It would be about why I got attacked, which would lead back to my family and the family legacy of violence and dirty money and Mikhail's connection to it. That wasn't a lid I wanted to open right now.

Plus me relating how I was grabbed from behind and struggled for all of two seconds before Mikhail burst through the door like Bruce Willis in *Die Hard*, although similar to what had happened to Samara, hardly compared to the terrifying experience Yelena had recently gone through. And the last thing I wanted to do was make either of them relive their own trauma right now. We could save that for another time over lots and lots of martinis.

Instead, I focused on what happened afterward, and Mikhail's complete, jaw-dropping reversal on how he treated me.

Yelena clapped when I got to the part about the dildo. "Oh my God, you *are* a dirty girl. I can't believe you swallowed that."

"Seriously, Nadia, way to break down stereotypes about shy virgins," Samara chimed in.

"As if either of you are ones to talk," I protested.

Samara and Yelena exchanged a look and laughed.

Yelena asked, "When is his birthday?"

"I don't know. I doubt he does either. They left him at an orphanage in Siberia. I don't think they kept substantial records."

Yelena thought for a moment, then said, "I bet he was born in April or May. He sounds like a Taurus. It's an earth sign. They are extremely stubborn, like bulls, but loyal to a fault."

That sounded like Mikhail.

She continued, "You know, when Taurus and Leos get together, it is an extremely sexual combination. They're both intense signs who channel anger and fights into highly charged, super kinky sex."

Now that part *really* sounded like Mikhail and me.

I threw the pillow I was holding back at her. "You added the super kinky part."

She shrugged. "Still true."

I crumbled the yellow waxy paper in my hand into a tiny ball. "It may not even matter…."

I told them about the surveillance cameras and how after finally being allowed to leave Gregor's house, I'd thought I was independent, but I really had never been.

Samara reached over and stroked my arm. "We never really apologized for what you suffered because of us running away."

I grabbed her hand and squeezed it. "No, don't say that. It really was for the best. When Gregor demanded I move in here, it was out of anger at first, but that quickly changed. He knew I hated living with my mother and all her constant backhanded remarks about how I dressed and what a waste of time it was to pursue a career in jewelry design. Gregor's the one who encouraged me to take jewelry making classes."

Samara smiled. "He appears to be this terrifying grizzly bear, but he has his teddy bear moments."

"He also insisted I take business classes so I would be ready when I wanted to open my own boutique."

"That sounds like him, too. He wants me to do the same. He wants me to take more art classes but is insisting on business ones too."

Yelena chimed in. "Damien's so supportive of me launching a fashion career, I'm a little afraid if I took any classes, he'd insist on going with me. I can see him now yelling at my teacher for giving me a low grade for a scalloped-edged collar I put on a dress."

I thought of Mikhail. I wish I could be certain he'd be as supportive of me as my brothers were of them. So far, I'd been in a relationship with him for less than twelve hours, and all I'd seen was his overbearing 'my rules or nothing' attitude. He'd also repeatedly brushed aside my concerns about my shop as if they were secondary to his own concerns about my safety. On one hand, I understood, but on the other it was sending up huge red flags. I voiced my concerns to Samara and Yelena.

All three of us were quiet for a moment. Finally, Yelena spoke. "I think there is only one solution to know the truth. Nadia, I think it's past time you ran away from home."

My mouth dropped open. "What?"

Samara jumped off the bed and grabbed me by the shoulders, raising me up. "It's the perfect plan! You need to run away."

I looked from one to the other. "You're both crazy."

"It worked for us," Yelena offered.

"How?" I protested. "You both wound up with the very men you were running from!"

Samara placed a hand over her belly. She wasn't showing yet. It was way too soon. "Sometimes you need to experience what you only think you want, to recognize what you truly want."

Yelena gave me a quick hug. "We're saying this because we love you. You need to leave. See what the world would be like without your brothers or Mikhail in it."

"Even if I wanted to, they would never give me permission to get on a plane and go somewhere completely alone. They'd freak out about security."

Samara winked. "Who says you're asking for permission?"

The idea sent a frisson of both fear and excitement

down my spine. I was twenty-one for heaven's sake, why shouldn't I travel and see the world? I had money to do it. I had inherited money from my father at his death. It was nothing compared to the tens of millions of dollars my brothers and apparently Mikhail had, but it was still a couple million. The only reason I didn't own the building where I had my apartment and shop was because they wanted to shield the Ivanov name by purchasing it through a shell company. I rarely spent any of my money because I didn't need to. I liked my secondhand furniture, off-the-rack babydoll dresses, and nights in watching movies. Still, maybe it was time to do something bold and rash on my own.

Maybe it *was* time to run away from home.

At the very least, it would give me space and time away from Mikhail. I needed to think about him and us. If I stayed here, I would never have a moment to think straight in his presence. He was just too intense, too sexy and overwhelming. I would forever happily submit to his will.

Yelena put her hands on her hips. "Well, if you're going to run away, we first need to get out of this room."

"I'm not leaving this second."

"I know. I just want to show them they didn't really lock us in here. Samara, pull the covers off the bed and grab that sheet." Yelena marched over to the window and threw up the sash.

I followed her and looked out. Just below there was a small balcony. She pointed to it. "The sheet will get me to the balcony. Once I'm there, you untie it and toss it down to me. I'll then retie it to the balcony and shimmy down the rest of the way to the ground."

Samara approached us with the end of the sheet. "It's anchored to the bedpost," she said before tossing it out the window.

Yelena shrugged out of the paisley silk robe she was wearing so she was only in her matching silk pajamas. She leaned down and threw her right leg over the sill. Samara grasped the sheet, braced her left foot against the wall and tightened her grip.

I watched them both in awe. "Why do I get the feeling this isn't the first time you're doing this?"

They both laughed. Yelena pointed to Samara. "The first time in Los Angeles was her fault."

Samara countered, "Yeah, but the second and third time in Mexico was all on you."

A stab of jealousy pierced my chest. I envied the bond they now had from their shared adventure. They were right. The only place I had ever traveled was to Russia, and that was always with family and under heavy guard. Maybe it was time I saw a bit of the world on my own. Maybe it was past time I had my own adventures.

Yelena slowly lowered herself to the balcony and then waved back. I helped Samara untie the sheet. We tossed it down to her. In only a few minutes, Yelena was running to the other side of the house, keeping close to the perimeter. It was only a few minutes later when we heard a muffled conversation on the other side of the door. We both jumped back when the door rattled, then there was the sound of something sliding against it followed by a dull thud.

The door swung open, with a beaming Yelena on the other side. We had to step over the guard when we exited.

Yelena shook her head. "Poor Carl disagreed with our plan. He'll be okay. He'll wake up in a few hours with a bump on his head and a bruised ego."

Samara straightened her shoulders. "Ladies, shall we adjourn to the kitchen for some hot chocolate and further planning of *Operation Fly the Coop?*"

This was happening. I was going to run away. A sudden chill settled over my fevered excitement.

What was Mikhail going to do when he realized I was gone?

CHAPTER 21

Mikhail

We parked our vehicle one street over so as not to draw attention on the quiet street we were targeting, especially since it was still morning. We didn't want to wait for the cover of darkness. At night, people in our line of work tended to be more on their guard. Not so much during the day. No one expected an attack in broad daylight, which was precisely why we were doing it now. Plus, we still had the element of surprise. Word would not have gotten to Dumb and Dumber yet of their crew's complete failure and our response.

It was only the three of us. This was going to be quick and deadly efficient. We did a perimeter sweep first. Novikoff's house sat on some property about twenty minutes outside of D.C.

The neighborhood was an odd mixture of quaint one-story pillbox houses built in the fifties and massive new McMansions squeezed onto every square inch of small half acre plots. It happened a lot. Grandma died, and her grandkids put her house up for a song just to unload it. Some asshole with money swoops in and buys it. First thing he does is tear it down and build some obnoxious monstrosity that casts a shadow over the surrounding houses.

Egor Novikoff was one of those assholes.

We made our way toward the obnoxious mansion. Taking up a position in the bushes of the small house next door, we watched for signs of activity. Several men patrolled the perimeter of the house, their sharp eyes scanning the space just above our hiding place.

Motioning with his hand, Gregor whispered, "That's our target."

I focused on a brick wall which spanned about twelve feet. On either side were two curtained windows. I could see through the white linen the faint impression of bookshelves and a desk. Egor's office.

I took out the Range-R. Cupping my hand to shield the bright screen, I tried to take a reading.

"We're too far away," I whispered.

Typically, the Range-R needed to be close to the target to take an accurate reading. Ideally, it would be pressed against the wall of the room it needed to scan. I had hoped our sniper position, barely one hundred yards away, would have sufficed. There was no way I could creep closer, take a reading, then get back into position to take the shot without possibly attracting the notice of the guards. They would be immediately suspicious of a man lurking near the house, but maybe not two men returning home drunk to their wives.

I motioned to Gregor and Damien. "I have an idea. Who's got a flask on them?"

Both Gregor and Damien pulled out beat-up silver flasks. I snatched Damien's, opened it, and poured some over Gregor's shirt and suit jacket.

"What the fuck," they objected practically in unison.

Gregor complained in a harsh whisper, "This was a nice suit."

Damien grimaced. "That was Macallan Rare scotch, aged over twenty years. Why couldn't you have grabbed Gregor's flask?"

"Because his has some decent vodka in it, not the swill you like to drink."

Damien shook his head. "You're both heathens with no appreciation for the finer things."

Gregor loosened his tie. "Let's do this."

Moments later, slurring his words, Gregor criss-crossed over the lawn, supported by Damien's shoulder. He called out, "Honey! Don't be mad. Let me in."

"Open up, Debbie, he didn't mean it," whined Damien in a sing-song voice.

Several guards came running, guns drawn.

"Sweet cheeks, is that you?" Gregor asked with an intentional blank look on his face.

"What the fuck is this?" asked one guard.

"A couple of drunk idiots," answered another.

As the guards circled around Gregor, he grabbed his stomach and hunched his shoulders. "I think I'm going to be sick!"

The guards immediately took several steps back, giving him a wide berth.

On unsteady legs, he lurched toward the bushes, leaning against the house's brick wall. He dry heaved several times.

The guards were so busy turning their heads in disgust, they didn't see the small handheld device he pressed against the wall.

Giving one last guttural gag for effect, he straightened.

"I feel better now." Looking about him, Gregor whined, "This isn't my sweet cheeks' house."

Damien slapped him on the back. "Come on, buddy. You can sleep it off at my place."

Without sparing the guards another glance, they walked away, making sure to wobble and sway as they went. They walked straight past my hiding place and made it look like they were entering the house next door.

I crouched low and peeked around the corner. The guards had dispersed. My plan had the added benefit of the guards now being reluctant to patrol on that side of the house because of the imaginary vomit in the bushes. Staying on my knees, I crawled back into position.

I focused on the Range-R through my scope to get a reading. It showed the outline of two seated figures pressed against the wall. Leonid and Lenin. Our intel reports had repeatedly confirmed the brothers spent a considerable amount of time alone in their father's office whenever he was out of town. There was speculation they were trying to open a safe he kept in there. I was certain it was the two of them, regardless of what they were doing. No one else in their organization would have a key to that room while Egor was out of town.

I would have to take them out with two rapid succession shots through the brick wall. My Mossberger 500 was fitted with an FPSRussia Salvo-12 suppressor, but unfortunately, it would barely muffle the sound. I kept my body still, knowing the slightest movement would draw attention to our position, and lined up the shot. I couldn't use a laser sight, so I had to do it by instinct. I held my breath as I braced for the impact and loud report.

I fired two shots, watching as shards of brick burst from the wall in a cloud of dust and noise. My gaze shifted to the Range-R. Both figures slumped forward. I didn't need to confirm the kill. Those two bullets were for Nadia, and I had never been more certain of a shot in my life. Those bastards were dead.

We bolted from our hiding place. We were out of range when we heard the cry of alarm and the sound of several Glocks firing at once. Once we were in the car driving away, Gregor sent an encrypted message to Egor Novikoff. He sent the video of Bruiser confessing to their involvement in Nadia's kidnapping attempt with a follow up text, boldly letting him know we had killed his only two sons and suggesting he not return to the United States.

After several minutes, he got a one-word response from Egor. *Understood.*

Damien leaned back in his seat. "Egor's an old man. He knew his sons were useless idiots. There was no way he was going to pass the business on to them."

I gripped the steering wheel. The adrenaline still ran

hot in my veins. "Will we need to worry about any retaliation?"

Gregor shook his head. "No. This time, it's really over. No one in that organization, obviously their father included, thinks those two are worth a war with us."

Damien rubbed his jaw. "I don't know about that. They had a sister."

I navigated through D.C. traffic. That was a problem for another day. Right now, I wanted to get back and check on Nadia and figure out how the hell I was going to tell her I burned down her dream.

CHAPTER 22

Mikhail

WHEN WE RETURNED to Gregor's house, we found the girls in the kitchen, but Nadia was missing.

"Where's Nadia?" I demanded harshly before anyone could say anything.

I realized my error, as Gregor and Damien exchanged a hard look. I had neutralized the danger and the premises was once again secure. There was no more threat, at least no more than usual. I had no reason to be demanding to know the whereabouts of their little sister.

Yelena broke the tension. "She decided to take a little nap. Apparently, she didn't get much sleep last night."

Ignoring her hidden jibe, I opened the refrigerator and grabbed a bottle of water. I wasn't really thirsty, but I needed to break Gregor's intense scrutiny. He had been watching my reactions to Nadia since we returned from her shop earlier. I was certain he suspected the change in our relationship. I would tell him soon. I just wanted to see Nadia first.

Damien strolled up to Yelena and gave her blonde curls a playful tug. With a resigned sigh, he asked, "Out the window?"

She lifted her chin and smiled. "You didn't seriously think locking the bedroom door and posting one silly guard on the other side was going to work?"

"It did at first."

She waved a hand in dismissal. "That's just because we wanted to finish our Cafe Mochas while they were still hot."

He leaned down and placed a kiss on her lips, before loudly whispering against them, "Next time, I'm tying you to the bed."

She scoffed. "With ropes?"

He bit her lower lip. "No, chains."

Gregor wrapped his arms around Samara's middle. He nuzzled her neck. "That's not a bad idea."

Samara gasped. "There better not be a next time, husband. You're lucky I didn't follow Yelena out that window and keep running."

"You try to run, and I'll hunt you down, wife," he playfully growled back, "and there will be consequences when I find you."

Turning away from the intimate banter between the couples, I muttered, "I'm going upstairs and grabbing a shower. I can't have me or my car reeking of gasoline if the cops come asking questions."

Plus, telling Nadia I burned down her beloved jewelry

store and apartment would be difficult enough without actually smelling like the deed. As I turned to go, Samara caught up with me. "She's in the blue suite."

My brow furrowed. That was my usual room. It wasn't unusual for me to crash here, especially after an event or if there was a situation. I had stayed just last week when that warlord from Afghanistan was in several all-night meetings with Gregor and Damien over a lost shipment of surface-to-air missiles a rival faction had confiscated. I usually kept a change of clothes and some personal items in the room. Nadia always stayed in the yellow suite whenever she visited Gregor. It had been her room a few years ago when she'd moved in with him after the girls ran off. Samara knew this.

At my confused look, she just shrugged and returned to Gregor's side.

I climbed the stairs and made my way down the carpeted hallway. I placed my hand on the doorknob to the blue suite and took a deep breath before slowly turning it. I pushed the door open and stepped inside the dimly lit room, closing the door behind me. The heavy watery blue satin curtain was pulled tightly closed; only a sliver of golden sunlight illuminated the mostly darkened room. After my eyes adjusted to the low light, I spied a small bundle curled up on the bed.

The tight fist in my chest loosened, and I took my first deep breath since leaving her side. There was no reason to suspect it, but I was half suspicious Samara and Yelena had lied about Nadia sleeping. Part of me panicked that she had snuck off in defiance of me. Approaching the bed on silent feet, I looked down at her sleeping form. She was on her right side with her right hand curled up next to her chin. She had taken off her heavy boots and socks. Her cute toes had a bright green glitter nail polish on them. Her lips were slightly open and there was the barest hint of a warm flush to her cheek. Her strawberry blonde hair took on more of a reddish hue in the soft light, which gave her skin an ivory glow.

She was so damn beautiful. It still amazed me how little she was aware of her own appeal. She was such a charming bundle of contradictions. Sweet, but with a sassy mouth. Innocent and shy but adventurous and bold as hell in bed. I brushed a curl off her shoulder and smiled as I thought back to earlier today. Never in a million years would I have guessed my sweet kroshka had a tendency to throw things when she was angry. She was so adorable when she was mad. Her eyes lit up and her small hands curled into cute tiny fists. I couldn't help but think she looked like Tinker Bell. I half expected a shower of gold dust to appear around her head as she stomped her feet.

Careful not to disturb the bed, I leaned over and pulled on the coverlet, lifting it over her sleeping form. Not wanting to awaken her, I crept across the room to the attached bathroom. I'm sure if they knew I had decided to shower in the same suite where she was sleeping, it would cause a stir with her brothers, but I didn't give a damn. They would know soon enough that I would not give her up without a fight.

Opening the glass double doors, I reached past the black marble tile and turned the silver handle. Scorching water showered down from the extra-large rectangular shower head which stretched across the length of the glassed-in chamber. I pulled off my shirt and unzipped my cargo pants as I kicked off my loosely laced boots before stepping into the already steaming shower.

Resting my palms against the cool tile, I let the water stream down my back, trying to erase the tension from the last twenty-four hours. It would still take some time for my body to know that the danger had passed. Blood still pulsed high and fast in my veins. It was always this way after a kill, but especially after this one. Never in my life did I regret taking a life less than the lives I had taken today. They had come too close to hurting Nadia, and I was glad they paid for it with their lives. My only regret was I couldn't look Leonid and Lenin in the eye as I shot them dead.

As I reached for the liquid soap, the bathroom door slammed open. Nadia stood on the threshold. She stormed in, grabbing the smooth silver handle to one of the glass shower doors before she swung it open. "How could you?"

Taken off guard, I didn't answer at first.

"How could you?" she repeated. Her light blue eyes filled with tears.

Fuck.

She gestured behind her. "I woke up and went downstairs. They didn't know I was in the hallway. I heard them talking about burning down my shop."

Brushing the water out of my eyes, I said, "Baby, I can explain."

Her pretty face crumpled. "No! No! No! How could you? How could you?"

She launched herself at me, pounding her fists on my

naked chest.

"I loved that shop. You had no right!"

I took a step back, holding my arms high, allowing her to hit me. I deserved it. It was no good explaining the reasons we'd had to burn it. She shouldn't be expected to be understanding about the situation. She had every right to be angry. I knew how hard she worked to make the shop a success. The long hours spent at her workbench working on custom jewelry pieces. The countless street festivals and fairs she attended to develop a fan base. She had even painted and decorated the main area herself, refusing help from anyone. It had been her dream, her own little slice of independence, a way to establish herself outside her brothers' shadows, and I had burned it to the ground.

She followed me into the shower, still striking me with her fists. The hot water drenched her hair and clothes, but in her anger, she didn't seem to notice or care. In an effort to calm her, I cupped her face. "Please, kroshka, listen to me."

She shook her head, jerking free of my grasp. I tried again, wrapping my hands around the sides of her neck and stepping close. Her fingernails clawed at my forearms. I stepped forward again, pressing her back against the tiles. With the pads of my thumbs, I pressed up on her jaw, forcing her head back.

Her lips quivered. "I hate you."

My eyes narrowed. I was desperately trying to be a good man, trying to understand her pain, but every primal instinct in my body howled to life at hearing those words from her beautiful mouth. She could be angry with me. She could hit me. She could even throw things at my head, but I couldn't bear hearing her say she hated me. That was something I just wouldn't tolerate.

Forcing my thigh between her legs, I pinned her to the shower wall. I lifted her arms high over her head, then interlaced my fingers with hers. I silenced her scream of protest with my mouth. My tongue swept in to claim hers. It had only been a few hours since I kissed her last, and already I craved and missed the taste of her. From this point forward, kissing her would be the very substance of my life, a need as great as food or air. She struggled, but I held firm. I pushed the top of my thigh against her cunt, swallowing her reluctant moan.

The scalding water pounded against my back, drenching us both. Impatient with the feel of her sodden turtleneck instead of her warm wet skin, I broke the kiss. Rearing back, I grabbed the hem of her shirt and whipped it over her head. She hadn't bothered to put her bra back on. Her full breasts were on display. With a cry, she lowered her arms and tried to cover herself. I snatched a fistful of her hair and pulled her head back, priming her for another kiss. As my mouth descended, I pushed her arms away, palming one perfect breast. I rolled one blush pink nipple between my fingers as I nipped and bit at her lower lip.

Still, she tried to fight me, turning her head at every opportunity, denying me.

"Open for me, baby," I breathed against her mouth.

"I can't. You've ruined everything," she moaned.

Lowering to my knees before her, I wrapped my arms around her hips and kissed the soft wet skin of her belly.

"Kroshka, believe me, I will spend the rest of my life making this up to you. You have my word."

Almost against her will, her hands hesitantly grasped my shoulders.

Reaching between us, I unbuttoned her cargo pants and lowered the zipper. I knew she hadn't put on a bra but was pleased to see my naughty girl had dared to go commando as well. I lowered the pants past her bare feet and tossed the heavily soaked fabric aside. Placing my hands on the tops of her thighs, I eased her legs open further. Her feet slid along the slick tile to obey me. I opened her nether lips and leaned in to flick the tip of my tongue over her swollen clit.

Nadia's fingers dug into my shoulders. "Oh, God."

I flicked her clit again, then swirled it around and around, feeling her body respond to my touch. Reaching a hand between her legs, I pushed one finger inside, then a second, opening her. I was careful to go slow, knowing she would still be sore from earlier, but also knowing my dirty girl liked a spike of pain with her pleasure. It was one of the things that made her the absolute perfect match for me.

I didn't realize I had said those words out loud till her body stiffened. Her hands pushed at my shoulders. "No. We aren't a match. You're nothing like I thought you'd be."

She tried to slide along the wet wall away from me, but my grip on her hip prevented her.

I rose to my full height, towering over her. "Well then, you're just going to have to get used to me, baby, because I'm not letting you go," I growled with more ferocity than I'd intended.

I knew I sounded like the overbearing Neanderthal she'd accused me of being, but I didn't care. I couldn't let her anger impede our future, not when I finally had her in my arms after all these years.

Her eyes narrowed. "Are you saying I don't have a choice in the matter?"

I placed a palm on the tile over her head and leaned down, coming within a breath of her lips. "That's exactly what I'm saying."

Her hand flew up to slap me. She was too slow.

I snatched her wrist and twisted her around till her front pressed against the marble.

"Let me go," she cried out.

Titling my head to the side, I sunk my teeth into the soft flesh of her neck, before licking the slight red outline of my bite mark. "Never."

I kicked at her feet, spreading her legs wide. Palming her cunt from behind, I pressed the tips of my two middle fingers against her clit. The slight pressure would only take the edge off her rising pleasure. To truly ease the ache, she'd need to feel the press of my thick cock inside of her. To taunt her body further, I swiped the pad of my thumb over her small, puckered hole.

She hissed as her body stiffened.

If I were a real bastard, I'd grab that liquid soap, pour some between the crack of her cute cheeks and fuck her ass till she screamed for mercy. With the last shred of civility I possessed, I restrained myself. While I may make her pussy sore from another relentless pounding so soon after taking her virginity, it would still be a pleasurable, delicious kind of soreness. Not so if I took her ass again so soon. She was just too tiny. I might harm her, especially in the hate fuck mood I was in right now.

Fisting my shaft, I pumped my hand several times, deliberately brushing my knuckles against her lower back. Her arms swept up the tiled wall, fingers splayed.

Lowering my knees slightly for leverage, I pressed the head of my cock at her entrance. The ridge of my shaft popped inside her tight hole. With my hands around her hips, I pulled them out till her ass brushed my lower abdomen and her back arched. The movement pushed my shaft into her another inch.

I wrapped my arm around her stomach and dipped my hands between her legs. Finding her clit, I pinched it hard between my finger and thumb as my other hand pressed down between her shoulder blades, forcing her into a submissive, vulnerable position. "I want to watch this tight pussy of yours swallow every fucking inch of my cock."

Nadia threw her head back and moaned.

I leaned over her, both of our bodies slick from the water beating down on us. "You're mine, Nadia, and I'm going to make sure you feel it and never forget it."

With that, I thrust in deep.

Her knees buckled but I held her upright. Her tight walls clamped down on my cock as I speared into her repeatedly, pounding into her tiny body, releasing all my anger and fear and love.

"Oh, God! Oh God! Mikhail!" she breathed as her body jerked forward with each of my thrusts.

Lifting my free hand, I brought my palm down on her ass. Her wet skin gave off a satisfying smack the moment I made contact. Heightened by the warmth of the shower, her cheek immediately glowed a bright cherry red. I spanked her again and again, matching each strike with a pulse of my hips as I thrust in deep to her core.

I was a man possessed. Needing her to not only hear my words but feel the possession of my body to know she was now mine alone.

Her fingers curled against the tiles as her body tensed. Her back arched, and her lips opened in a silent scream. I could feel the spasms from her orgasm ripple up my shaft. Once she had achieved her release, I thrust into her with abandon, needing her to feel every thick inch as the waves of pleasure crested then crashed over her body. My balls tightened. The pressure was almost painful. Finally, my head fell back as I let out a roar of completion, releasing deep into her body, selfishly praying my seed took hold.

Pulling free, I swung her around and clasped her to me. I enclosed her in my arms and pressed her head to my chest. Still breathing hard, I rasped against the top of her head, "Take it back."

Her hands slid up my sides to wrap high around my back, but she remained silent.

I grasped her tighter and repeated, "Take it back."

She lifted her gaze and stared at me for a moment. "I don't hate you. I could never hate you."

"And?"

"And... I'm yours, Mikhail."

I lowered my head and claimed her mouth, wanting to taste the sweet truth of her words. Ruthlessly pushing aside the bitter doubts which tried to warn me she was lying.

CHAPTER 23

Mikhail

WITH NADIA TUCKED naked in bed fast asleep, I went in search of her brothers. It was time we came to an understanding. Now that the danger had passed, I wanted to bring Nadia back to my penthouse. I wanted her in my bed tonight and every night from now on.

As I walked downstairs, the house was quiet and still.

After searching the kitchen and living room, I found Gregor in his study. He was standing over his desk with his palms on the surface, studying a large map with a pile of files next to it. He was so engrossed he didn't look up right away. On the bookshelf, there was a small brass clock whose relentless and solemn *tick tick tick* filled the silence.

Still without looking up, he motioned for me to come

closer. "Mikhail, I'm glad you're here. I want you to look at this."

I approached the desk and looked down. It was a detailed street map of Caracas, Venezuela.

Gregor straightened and reached for a folder on top of a stack. "One of our *friends* at the CIA has reached out and asked us to squash a bug."

I opened the folder. The man was basically a typical corrupt politician who was not above using violence against even women and children to secure his fortune. I nodded. "It's tough to take these assholes out. They have too much security for a close hit, and my Spanish is rusty at best."

Gregor took the folder back from me. "Agreed. Apparently, he's making a speech next month." He pointed to the Plaza Bolivar. "From a grandstand, here."

I raised an eyebrow. "A public assassination?" I looked over the map. Tapping a finger over the location, I said, "Here. The Catedral de Caracas. It's your best bet for a sniper's nest with the highest vantage point."

Gregor nodded in agreement as he crossed to the sideboard where the housekeeper had set out an elaborate Lomonosov sterling silver and cobalt blue enamel samovar which I had no doubt had been in their family for generations. Lifting the gilded handle of a podstakannik, he released the samovar spout and poured hot black tea into the glass, added two lumps of sugar and handed it to me. The distinct campfire scent unique to traditional Russian Caravan tea wafted around the room. He then lifted a small tray of cookies, candies, and lemon cakes, but I waved him off.

He fixed his own glass and returned to the desk. "I'm thinking you could use the Barrett M82."

I shrugged. It was a decent sniper rifle, but the Lobaev SVL would be better. I told him so. "That shot has to be at least twelve hundred meters if they put the stage facing north, which is the most likely location. The Lobaev SVL is more accurate at that distance."

"Yes, but we don't have thirty crates of Lobaev SVLs that we're trying to sell to a warlord in the Sahel region."

I agreed. "Good point. Blowing a guy's head off from over a thousand meters away would be an effective sales presentation of the Barrett M82 capabilities."

Gregor took a sip of his tea, then said, "Good. I'll cut you in for fifty percent since you'll be handling the *sales presentation* for this one. You'll also get the usual seventy-five percent cut of the CIA's shadow fee."

I nodded. "Just have them send the money into the usual account, and I'll transfer over your portion." After a pause, I asked, "Where is everyone?"

Gregor walked back to the sideboard and picked up a small sugar cookie, probably one left over from the wedding ransom. It was hard to believe that celebration was only yesterday. It felt like a lifetime ago, so much had changed and happened.

Gregor returned to the desk. "Damien took Yelena back to their place, but he'll be back to review our Venezuela plans. Samara is in … bed… resting." Knowing Gregor, I'm sure she needed the *rest*.

He continued, "And I assume, Nadia is still upstairs napping."

The room fell silent.

Tick, tick, tick.

Taking a deep breath, I said, "About Nadia— "

Damien breezed into the room, announcing, "That woman will be the death of me."

He crossed over to the samovar and picked up a glass, releasing the spout to fill it with hot tea. As the glass heated up, he immediately had to shake his hand, then he grabbed a podstakannik and dropped it into the ornate metal-handled holder. Tossing a numbingly sweet four sugar cubes into his tea, he joined us at the desk. "She climbed outside that damn window in her freaking pajamas."

I offered, "Next time lock her in a bedroom with clothes."

Gregor grimaced. "The point of locking her in a guest bedroom without access to clothes was to prevent an escape."

Damien shook his head as he took a bite of a kefir cookie. "Right out the fucking window. Damn, I love that woman."

Gregor tapped the map. "Mikhail's good with the plan."

Damien set his tea aside. "You'll have to use the Barrett M82 not the Lobaev SVL. You good with that too?"

I nodded. "We already discussed it. Makes sense. I'll make it work."

Again, the room fell silent.

Damien and Gregor exchanged a look.

I pushed my shoulders back as I straightened, sensing the rising tension in the room.

Gregor cleared his throat. "We need to talk about Nadia."

Shifting my gaze between the two of them, I took a step back as Damien rose out of his seat and crossed his arms over his chest.

Tick, tick, tick.

Gregor walked around behind his desk and crossed toward the far-right bookshelf where, I happened to know, behind a false front of leather-bound Tolstoy novels there was a wall safe with a loaded Para 1911 G.I. Expert handgun next to it.

On the other side of the desk, I eased casually backward to lean against another bookshelf. Under some old gun magazines on the shelf behind me, I had a CZ P-10 F striker-fired pistol hidden. It was a simple gun with a polymer frame, which made it ideal for concealment and close quarter kills.

Gregor had hidden his gun behind the books, because going for a weapon in a desk drawer was an obvious move which clients and enemies, usually both one and the same, would easily expect and be watching for. I had a gun hidden in this room because it was my job to always be prepared.

Tick, tick, tick.

I weighed my words carefully. "Yes, it's past time we talked about Nadia."

Damien released a long breath. "After what happened last night, I think we are all in agreement she needs to marry. The sooner, the better. It will take the target off her back. The alternative is forcing her to move back in with Gregor where she can be watched and protected twenty-four seven, and I think we all know how that plan would be received."

Gregor's hand slid along the leather bindings. There was a soft click as the latch keeping the false front in place released. "As we've said before, it will need to be someone suitable. We can't allow just anyone to marry into the Ivanov family." He flipped the bindings down, exposing the safe and the gun.

My fingertips slid along the glossy surface of the top magazine. "I agree."

Fuck.

They knew.

They at least knew something, probably not all the details, but they knew something had happened between me and Nadia. They knew the situation had changed. If they disapproved and tried to challenge my claim on their sister, then I faced an impossible choice.

This couldn't be happening. Gregor and Damien weren't just my employers, they were my closest friends. I didn't want bloodshed. What kind of future would Nadia and I have if I built our marriage on the blood of her family? The Ivanov name didn't just belong to her brothers. They had extended family in Chicago, Russia, and London, all in the mafia game. They would hunt us down. Nowhere would be safe. She'd be in constant danger, more so than now. Now, she was only the occasional target of an opportunist. If I killed her brothers and we fled, she'd be wanted by every member of her family. They would hunt her down and make an example of her, blood or no blood.

And that was only if I could convince her to come with

me. I loved Nadia with every breath in my body and despite her protestations earlier, I knew she loved me, but that would change if I killed her brothers. I'd forever be a monster in her eyes. I'd destroy her and us.

I couldn't do it.

I loved her too much.

I loved her enough to let her go.

I loved her enough to die for her.

I pulled my hand back, away from my hidden gun. If Gregor reached for his and killed me for betraying him by going after his sister, then so be it. I wouldn't defend myself. I couldn't do that to Nadia.

Gregor's hand moved toward the gun.

Tick, tick, tick.

His hand shifted to the wall safe where he punched in a seven-digit code. The safe door sprung open. He reached inside and turned toward me. In his hand was a small red velvet box.

My entire body braced, unsure of what was happening or what would happen next.

Tick, tick, tick.

Gregor tossed the velvet box to me. I caught it and flipped open the lid. Inside was a vintage Art Deco diamond and emerald ring, similar to the style which inspired Nadia's jewelry designs.

He walked over to Damien and clapped him on the shoulder. They both turned their heads and smiled at me. Gregor gestured to the ring. "You don't have to, but we think you should use her great-grandmother's engagement ring when you propose. She's always loved it."

What?

They both crossed the room and slapped me on the back at the same time. I pitched forward slightly from the impact as I tried to force my mind to catch up.

Damien laughed. "Look at this face! He thought you were going to put a bullet in him."

Gregor patted my back a second time. "Get used to that shellshocked, kicked in the gut feeling my friend. Based on my experience, that's marriage."

My brow furrowed. "I don't understand. You've made it clear for years that it wasn't possible. My lack of family, of a proper name. The Ivanov honor."

Gregor pushed the tea samovar aside and grabbed three glasses while Damien unscrewed the cap on a bottle of Stoli Elit Vodka. He poured three generous shots and passed them around.

I stared at the velvet ring box in my left hand as I clasped the vodka glass in my right. Nothing seemed real in this moment.

Damien clinked my glass. "We were wrong to think that, my friend. Life, and more importantly, love, has shown us just how wrong. You love our sister. That is all that matters and all that should have mattered.

Gregor raised his glass. "Za nashu druzhbu!" *To our friendship!*

We all drank.

Damien poured another round, although he shook his head. "I really don't know how you both drink this tasteless crap." He raised his glass and toasted, "Vyp'yem za lyubov'!" *Let's drink to love!*

Gregor placed his hand on my shoulder. His smile faded. "Although, I don't have to tell you. If you hurt her or make our sister unhappy—" He reached past me and lifted my handgun out from its hiding place under the stack of magazines. "We'll kill you."

I should have known better than to think I had gotten anything over on Gregor.

I tossed back half my vodka. "Don't worry. If that should happen, I'm pretty sure she'll be the one to pull the trigger."

Damien shrugged. "She's an Ivanov. To our baby sister!"

I raised my glass. "And my future wife."

Gregor advised, "You better marry her soon before someone else gets any stupid ideas."

I grinned. "Trust me, I've wasted enough time where Nadia is concerned. I have no intention of waiting any longer. If I have my way, we'll be married before the end of the week."

In that moment of celebration, it never occurred to any of us that Nadia might not agree to our immediate plans for her future wedded bliss.

CHAPTER 24

Nadia

MIKHAIL'S ARM wrapped around my waist from behind. He had laid down beside me, fully clothed on top of the covers. I snuggled into his embrace. My head hurt from trying to figure out all my mixed emotions, but in that moment, all I wanted was to feel his strength and warmth and believe everything was going to be okay.

He gently kissed the top of my head. "I promise, kroshka, I will fix this."

My lower lip trembled as my eyes filled with tears. I didn't want him to know I was crying, but I couldn't contain my shaky inhale.

With a muttered curse under his breath, he turned me to face him. Placing an arm under my head, he pulled me close, till my ear was pressed against his heart. I inhaled his sandalwood cologne scent. He also smelled faintly of my favorite tea, like an outdoor campfire on a winter's night, which was oddly comforting. His hand cradled my head as he held me close within his embrace.

"Please, baby, don't cry. I'll make it better. Trust me."

His plea only made me cry harder. I knew it was only a store. We could rebuild it. Samara, Yelena, and I had already been talking about doing a boutique gallery and store together anyway, so I probably would have switched locations in the coming months. Still, it was *my* store. It was something I'd accomplished on my own that I was very proud of, and now it was gone. I should have been, and was, happy everyone I loved was safe and did trust that it wasn't a decision Mikhail took lightly. I knew deep in my heart he and my brothers had their reasons. I knew none of them would have been so cruel and callous as to ruin my dreams if it wasn't absolutely necessary to protect me and the family, but it still stung.

Rubbing soothing circles on my back, he sang to me in a soft baritone. "Kak ya lyublyu glubinu tvoikh laskovykh glaz, Kak ya khochu k nim prizhat'sya khot' raz gubami! Tomnaya noch' razdelyayet, lyubimaya, nas, I trevozhnaya, chornaya step' prolegla mezhdu nami."

It was the bittersweet Russian love song, *Dark is the Night*. I had never heard him sing before. The effect was beautifully sad and mesmerizing.

He repeated the lyrics in English. "How I love the depths of your gentle eyes, How I want to press my lips to them! This dark night separates us, my love, And the dark, troubled steppe has come to lie between us."

I lifted my face up to his, and he kissed me. It wasn't one of his soul searing, forget-your-own name, possessive kisses. It was gentle, almost hesitant. His lips sought mine. He licked my bottom lip before running the tip of his tongue along the sharp edge of my teeth. His tongue swept in.

I groaned and opened my mouth wider as I twisted my fists into the fabric of his shirt.

It was all the encouragement he needed. He leaned into the kiss, taking firmer control. He shifted his hand to cup my jaw, pushing down with his thumbs to open my mouth further and deepen the kiss. The hard ridge of his lengthening cock pressed against my upper thigh through the covers. He shoved the blankets down to expose my breast. Breaking our kiss, he closed his lips around my nipple as his warm hand caressed down my back to grip my waist, holding me in place. He pulled on the delicate flesh, scraping it slightly with his teeth. I groaned as I gripped the hair at his nape.

"Bozhe, ty mne nuzhen, detka," he murmured against my skin.

I needed him, too. I couldn't even remember the time before he was in my life. I relied on and believed in his powerful presence, always there, always watching over and protecting me. He was my very own dark archangel. Still, this new insanely intense level to our relationship was terribly overwhelming. It caught me in a storm, spinning and spinning. The calm atmosphere of the eye may lull me, but I was still aware of the dangerous chaos he brought, swirling around me, threatening to destroy everything.

His hand swept over my hip, slipping beneath my knee. He pulled my leg up so he could press into my core.

"Oh, God!" I breathed as my head fell back.

This was insane. We'd already had sex several times, and yet I still craved more. The more he touched me, the more I needed him to fuck me. I didn't even recognize myself. I did not know I could even be such a reckless wanton. I was finally living up to my free-spirited fire zodiac sign and embracing my passionate side, and it scared the hell out of me.

He leaned back. "Let's get out of here."

I blinked, still caught in his sensual haze. "What?"

He licked my bottom lip. "I need you back in my bed, under my roof. Not here."

I pulled the blankets up to cover my breasts. "I can't just leave. They'll wonder where I went."

"They think you're up here napping. Come on."

"What if they notice I'm gone? They'll ask where I am."

"And I'll tell them you're with me."

The Leo in me whispered, *Do it. Why not?*

My head turned to stare at the entrance to the bathroom. My cheeks flamed at the memory of my attacking him in my grief and him fucking me senseless in the shower less than an hour earlier. "My clothes are all wet."

"I'll check the yellow suite," he offered. "Maybe you left something behind in there."

He returned a few minutes later. "I could only find this." He held up a cobalt blue short skirt with a small pink daisy pattern on it. "Wait." He walked over to one of the large cabinets which doubled as closets and opened it. He pulled out a white V-neck t-shirt. "Here. Arms up."

I kneeled up on the bed, letting the blanket slip to my hips, and obeyed. He pulled the shirt down my arms and over my head. Placing a hand around the nape of my neck, he untucked my riot of curls and fluffed them over my shoulders and down my back.

He took a step back and tilted his head as his gaze wandered over me.

I blushed at his scrutiny.

I was wearing his t-shirt.

It was such a *girlfriend-boyfriendy* thing to be doing.

This was precisely the kind of thing I thought of when I allowed myself to dream about being with Mikhail.

"It's a bit big," he pointed out.

I laughed. That was an understatement. What was probably a t-shirt on him was a dress that reached practically to my knees.

He pulled the fabric around my waist tight and knotted it. He smiled. "Much better."

I looked down and gasped. It was now pulled taut over my breasts, making them seem way bigger than they really were, and showing off my pink nipples through the thin white fabric. I covered my chest with my forearms. "I can't wear this!"

"Just be glad I'm letting you put the skirt on," he growled with a suggestive look between my legs.

I looked down and immediately dove under the covers and curled up on my side. I'd been so enthralled with watching him knot the fabric around my waist, I'd failed to notice that, with it bunched up, it exposed my pussy and ass.

Mikhail swatted my butt through the covers. "Come on. The house is quiet. Now's the time to make our escape."

I reached out and pulled the skirt over the covers and under the blanket with me. I wriggled into it, ignoring Mikhail's bemused expression.

"You know I've practically licked every inch of your body by now?"

"It doesn't mean I'm used to… to… whatever… *this* is," I exclaimed with a wave of my hand between the two of us.

Fully dressed, I finally emerged out from under the blankets. Mikhail grabbed my pink Doc Martens and knelt at my feet.

"I can do that," I objected.

He winked. "I know, but I want to do it."

He grasped one leg just beneath my knee and ran his hand down my calf to lift my foot. He pushed on one boot, letting it rest between his legs as he loosely laced it up. He then did the same with my other leg. Running his large warm hands over my skin, giving me goosebumps with every touch. How did this man have the power to turn such a mundane thing like putting on a pair of boots into something wicked? When he was finished lacing the second boot, he caressed the tops of my thighs, pushing his hands beneath the hem of my skirt. I held my breath. The tip of one fingertip caressed my pussy.

He leaned in close. "I love the fact only I will know my naughty girl is not wearing any panties."

Oh. My. God.

He grasped my hand and pulled me up. "Let's go home."

Home?
Did he say home?

Maybe it was just a figure of speech. I had enough on my plate without over-analyzing every little word or phrase that came out of the man's mouth, I cautioned myself.

He held onto my hand as we walked down the hallway. I tried to pull it back when we reached the stairs in case we encountered anyone on the lower level, but he only tightened his grip. An excited, illicit thrill fluttered in my stomach. We were playing with fire. If my brothers saw us, there would be hell to pay. It was like I was a teenager sneaking out with my bad boy boyfriend.

When we got to the entryway, Mikhail gave me a quick kiss on the forehead. "I'll go bring the car around."

As he left, I swiveled my head from left to right to make sure we weren't observed. The house seemed pretty quiet. Yelena and Damien had gone back to their place, and Samara was probably in her painting studio in the other wing to take advantage of the bright afternoon sunlight. I looked down the dark hallway to the right. I bit my lower lip in indecision. If Samara was in her studio, that meant Gregor might be alone in his study. It would be easier to talk to my brothers about Mikhail one at a time instead of trying to take them both on at once.

Peeking through the side window next to the front door, I didn't see Mikhail yet. He must have gotten waylaid going to his car. After taking a deep breath, I headed down the shadowed corridor. On one side were the disapproving, thin-lipped sneers of my ancestors, memorialized in somber browns and blacks surrounded by ornate gilt frames. On the other was one long tapestry in black and gold depicting a traditional stag hunt. Gregor was many things, but subtle was not one of them. Anyone who approached his study, or as I usually thought of it, his lair, knew precisely what they were getting into. The weight of the powerful Ivanov name on one side, a not-so-subtle warning of their hunting prowess on the other.

My heart was beating in my chest so loud I had to strain to hear if there were any noises coming from the study. Stopping just out of view, I tilted my head and listened. Nothing. This was so silly. Gregor was my brother. I loved him and he loved me. There was no reason to be nervous. Sure, he and Damien had actively discouraged any hope of a relationship between me and Mikhail for years, but there wasn't any reason to believe they would still be against it now that I was twenty-one and capable of making my own decisions.

My heart was beating so fast it was making me dizzy. I shook my hands in an effort to release the stiff tension in my fingers. I turned and stepped over the threshold. It took a moment for my gaze to focus on the space behind his desk and realize the room was empty. I released the breath I was holding in a huff.

On second thought, this was for the best. I should wait till I had a better idea what was happening between Mikhail and me before I talked with my brothers. It wasn't like we were in some rush to the altar or anything. It had barely been twelve hours since he kissed me for the first time in three years, for heaven's sake. I could stir up a bunch of shit, and it could all be for nothing. Mikhail could change his mind about us… or I could. This was all still crazy new and crazy insane. This could have just been shock from my near-death experience last night. Or stirred up emotions after seeing Samara and Gregor get married. That kind of thing happened at weddings all the time. People got all emotional and sentimental at seeing a couple in love and wanted that for themselves. It felt deeper, but what did I really know about boyfriends and love?

Mikhail and I needed time to just slow things down — way down. Maybe have a little fun dating in secret for a while, before we made any major decisions. It would give me time to get to know the real him, not this image of him I'd built up in my mind over the years.

I returned to the entryway to see Mikhail exiting the driver's side of the car. I walked out to greet him and smiled when I realized he had only gotten out so he could open the passenger door for me. He returned behind the wheel, and eased the car down the long, tree-lined driveway. I reached for the seat belt but then stopped and folded my hands in my lap, hoping maybe he would do *the move* again. A minute later, before we pulled out onto the busy neighborhood street, Mikhail leaned over and grabbed the shoulder strap of my seat belt and buckled me in.

I slipped my lips over my teeth to quell my smile. *Eek!* Buckling the seat belt for me was such a cute and sexy, girlfriend-boyfriendy thing for him to do. I leaned back into my seat and watched the houses go by as I imagined all the fun dating things we were going to do the next few months. I think I could definitely get used to calling Mikhail my boyfriend.

CHAPTER 25

Nadia

I BLINKED SEVERAL TIMES, certain I hadn't heard him right. "What do you mean we're getting married?"

It was frightening how quickly things went sideways.

It started when, after parking in his penthouse garage, Mikhail pulled a familiar-looking suitcase and purse out of the trunk.

I snatched up the black leather hobo bag and looked inside. My cellphone with the charger still attached was right on top. Underneath it was my wallet and now useless apartment and shop keys. I pointed to the small black carry-on bag. "Is that my suitcase?"

Mikhail nodded. "I only grabbed a few items from the boxes. We'll go back in a few days to grab the rest of your stuff."

Um, what?

When did we discuss me automatically spending the night here? Let alone moving in?

He grabbed my hand and led me onto the elevator. After punching in the security code, the doors closed, and it whisked us to the top floor. I watched the small numbers illuminate and used them as my version of counting to ten.

When we were inside his penthouse, Mikhail picked up my suitcase and walked toward the bedroom.

Tossing my purse on the kitchen counter, I tried to stop him. "You can just leave that in front... for now."

He raised an eyebrow and glanced at the entryway near the door where I pointed. Then, without saying a word, he turned and continued into the bedroom.

I paced a few times in the living room till I heard him in the kitchen.

He was slightly bent over pulling items out of the refrigerator. He had changed into a pair of silky-looking black workout pants and a slim fitting t-shirt. Damn, the man had the greatest ass. It was all hard and curved with that hollow divot on the side of each cheek. The t-shirt showed off all the amazingly colorful tattoos on his forearms and up his shoulders.

I swallowed. It was going to be really hard to focus.

He put some eggs, a tomato, and a small container of feta cheese on the counter. "Hungry? I'm not a great cook, but I can make a pretty mean omelette," he said with a wink.

Dammit. He was being all cute and sexy, boyfriendy right now. Maybe I was just over-analyzing this?

Shifting the crystal salt and pepper shakers across the

counters between my hands, I gathered my courage and tried to keep my voice casual. "What did you mean when you said 'get the rest of my stuff'?"

He glanced over his shoulder at me as he placed a skillet on the stovetop and turned the knob to medium-high heat. "You know, your clothes and stuff. Your things. I'm going to move the furniture out of the spare bedroom and set up a workshop for you in there. I figure that should work till I can find you a new space for your shop."

I grabbed the saltshaker so hard small red crescents formed on my palms from my nails. "Till *you* find *me* a space?"

He continued as if he hadn't even heard me. "Of course, we may want to wait till we find a house. We don't want your shop to be too far away from our home." He cracked several eggs into a bowl and whipped them with a fork.

What is happening?

I cleared my throat. "A house?"

He walked the few steps to where I was standing at the end of the marble-top kitchen island and gave me a quick kiss on my forehead. "Of course, kroshka, we can't stay here in the penthouse. You don't want to raise our children in a place without a yard to play in, do you?"

Children?

I rubbed my temples. "Am I missing something here? We've been together for twelve hours and have fought for half that time, and somehow you already have us with a house and two point five kids."

Mikhail stopped chopping the tomato and looked up at me. His blue eyes turned to hard cobalt. Still holding the knife, he stepped toward me. I instinctively backed up, staring at the bright silver blade. It was covered in small pieces of red that my brain knew was just tomato, but my heart leaped as if it were blood. His eyes narrowed at my movement.

Without saying a word, he reached over to turn off the stovetop. My chest tightened. That probably wasn't a good sign. He then slowly put down the knife. Cupping his right fist in his left palm, he cracked his knuckles and studied me a moment, inhaling deeply as if to calm himself down. Finally, he said, "You do realize that until you marry, you'll continue to be vulnerable to these types of attacks? That seizing you would essentially be a dangerous, opportunistic power grab against your brothers?"

Incredulous, I asked, "So I'm just supposed to marry the first guy who walks through the door because my brothers' business demands it?"

He slammed his fist down on the island. The jarring gesture made my heart leap into my throat. "No, not the first man. Me. We're getting married and that is all there is to it."

"What do you mean we're getting married? I haven't even told my brothers about us yet."

"I have." His gaze bore into mine, daring me to object.

My mouth dropped open. "You what?"

I was having a hard time keeping up with the steamroll job he was doing to my life. First, he was taking over my business operations, then talking about marriage, a house, and kids. It was like he and my brothers had planned out the rest of my life, and were just expecting me to be a good girl and follow along. Regardless of how I may have felt about Mikhail — and I hadn't really been given an opportunity to even figure that out — this was not okay. If I allowed this to happen, I could forget about any independence whatsoever. They would settle my life before I had had a chance to ever really live it, before I had a chance to make my own mistakes and my own decisions.

"Your brothers and I have already discussed it. This is for your own protection. It's all settled."

"Eto bylo dlya vashey zhe zashchity! Always for my own protection."

Mikhail started for me, but I pivoted out of his reach, keeping the island between us. He took a few more steps, and I did the same. A low feral growl emitted from deep within his chest. I was playing with fire and I knew it, but dammit, he couldn't just storm into my personal life and start ordering me around.

"You will obey me in this, kroshka."

"You can't just order someone to marry you."

"The hell I can't!" He lunged, but I was too quick. I circled around the island again, always keeping the large block of marble between us.

"Did it even occur to you or my brothers to ask me how I felt about this plan of yours?"

Judging by his closed off, hooded expression, the answer was no.

I crossed my arms over my chest. "I won't do it."

"Da, vy budete," he fired back.

"No, I won't," I insisted, "and you can't make me."

Mikhail's eyebrow raised. His lips twisted into a mirthless smirk. "Watch me."

"You know what, Mikhail—"

He lifted his arm and pointed a finger at me. "I'm warning you, babygirl, don't you fucking dare say it."

I paused but didn't think better of it. "Poshel na khuy!"

Placing his palm flat on the island surface, Mikhail swung his legs high and leapt over it.

I tried to run, but he grabbed a fistful of my hair and pulled me back till I was flush against his chest. I could feel the threat of his hard cock press against my ass. His hand wrapped around my throat, forcing my head back onto his shoulder as the tops of his fingers pressed under my jaw.

He took my earlobe between his teeth and bit before breathing into my ear, "Are you doing this on purpose, babygirl?" His hand reached down between my legs and cupped my pussy through the thin fabric of my skirt. "You think because I know this pussy is sore, I won't rough fuck punish you till you can't walk for a week?"

Oh. My. God.

There was something seriously wrong with me that such a freaking fucked up thing like that threat would actually make my nipples hard and my thighs clench. There was no denying I was deliberately provoking him. Poking the beast. I couldn't seem to help myself. There was this dizzying adrenaline rush the moment his brow lowered and his mouth tightened. His body would tense right before he sprang into motion.

This must be what people call the thrill of the chase.

I was still pissed about him colluding with my brothers about my future, but there were better ways to handle the situation than screaming 'fuck you' and practically daring him to hate fuck me into oblivion.

Mikhail spun me around and bent me over the kitchen island. The cold marble made my nipples even harder. His hand around my throat tightened, not enough to cut off my air, but just enough to be a darkly erotic threat. His other hand moved up the back of my thigh, under the hem of my skirt. He flipped up the fabric, exposing my bare hip and ass.

He rubbed his palm in circles over one cheek. "I haven't just watched *over* you these last few years. I've *watched* you, too. I know the feel of your eyes on me. I recognize the want and need in their depths because it has mirrored my own."

He smacked my ass. My mouth opened on a shocked gasp as my body tensed. The movement of my jaw tightened his grip on my throat. I shamefully rose on my toes and rubbed my ass against his cock.

He smacked my ass again. He leaned down to rasp in my ear, "I know how badly you hunger for this. I know you crave my touch — crave each brutal embrace. You can deny it all you want, babygirl, but you like being dominated by me. You fight me just so I will break you."

Shocked at the raw honesty of his words, I struggled to be free, but he tightened his grasp on my hip. My breath came in quick gasps as I tried to slow my beating heart, and I still denied it. "No. It's not true."

He brushed his hips against my ass before pressing the hard ridge of his cock between my cheeks. "You're lying. You've lain in bed countless nights wondering what it would be like to be pinned beneath my weight, struggling against my grasp on your wrists as I thrust my cock deep into your tight cunt, swallowing your screams with my mouth."

"Oh God," I whimpered as I pressed my thighs together, trying to ease the painful ache his wicked words were causing.

Still, he tormented me, his deep voice harsh and low. "I know because I've dreamed about it too. Every damn night for the last three years, I've gripped my cock and stroked, imagining you writhing beneath me. Your pretty lips still swollen from struggling to take my long shaft down your throat. Your long hair fanned out over my pillow. My hips between your thighs as I drive into your sweet heat over and over and over again till you cry out in pained pleasure from the assault."

I slipped one hand between my legs and rubbed my fingers through the slick arousal, using the tip to tease my clit, desperately needing to take the edge off my building orgasm. Fuck, this man had quite a hold over me if he could make me come just with the power of his words.

His teeth sank into my earlobe as the flat of his palm once more struck my ass. The sharp sting of pain made me cry out. I could feel the vibration of his growl along my back. "Say it. Say you're my dirty girl."

I squeezed my eyes tightly shut. "Please don't make me," I whispered past his grip on my throat.

He tightened his fingers. I went up on my toes as my hand gripped the edge of the marble island. He spanked my upper thigh and the curve just below my ass cheek. Hot needles radiated from my ass up my spine.

He repeated his dark command as his fingers pushed

mine aside. "Don't test me on this. I want you to say it. Say you're my dirty girl, and you'll obey me." He thrust two fingers into my still swollen and sore pussy.

Tears streaked down my cheeks as I submitted to him. Worse, as I found myself wanting to submit to him, needing to.

The pad of his thumb caressed my dark hole. His threat was clear. "Don't make your punishment worse than it needs to be, kroshka." He ran the tip of his tongue along the edge of my jaw. It was impossible not to imagine that same tongue licking and teasing my clit till I cried out in submission.

My tongue flicked out to wet my lips. Finally, I relented to the fierce pull of his power and strength over me. "I'm your… your… dirty girl."

He pushed a third finger inside of me as he pressed his thumb deeper into my ass, past the knuckle. My pussy burned as its already tortured walls stretched to accommodate his fingers, and I knew the pain would be so much worse when he forced his thick shaft inside of me. I moaned at the thought of him relentlessly driving into my bent over body as he gripped my throat harder and harder, cutting off my air, holding the power of life and death over me, demanding I come on his command.

He shifted his hand from my throat to my hair. Fisting it, he pulled my head back. "Not good enough, kroshka. Tell me what I want to hear."

My brain screamed not to say it, but my body begged me to utter the words he wanted to hear. In that moment, I would have done anything to stop his sexual torment. "I'll obey you."

Using his grip on the hair at the nape of my neck, he yanked me upright and around straight into his arms. His mouth claimed mine as his enormous hands wrapped around my waist and lifted me high to place me on the edge of the island countertop. I hissed as the heated skin of my ass from his spanking hit the cold marble surface. Wedging my thighs open, he stepped between them, grabbing my ankles and wrapping my legs around his lower torso. There was a rush of disappointment when I realized the island was too tall for me to feel the press of his cock between my legs.

His hands gripped my jaw as he pulled back and gazed deeply into my eyes. "This is for your own good, baby. You need to trust me. I know what's best for you."

The pad of his thumb swiped at the fresh tear which fell down my cheek. He continued, "I wouldn't be doing this if I didn't believe deep in my soul that we were meant to be together. I know it, kroshka, as I know the certainty of my next breath. With me, you will be protected and want for nothing."

He lowered his head, but just as his lips touched mine, his cellphone went off. Glancing at the screen, he cursed and answered it. He barked orders in rapid Russian. He slammed the phone down and drew a frustrated hand through his hair. "I have to leave, but I'll return in a few hours."

"Are my brothers okay? Samara? Yelena?"

He stroked my cheek with the back of his knuckles. "Yes, baby. They are fine. This is a different matter that requires my... special touch."

Mafia. Illegal. Dangerous. Criminal. Murder.

The words tripped across my brain like rapid gunfire.

He lifted me off the island and kept his hands on my waist till my wobbly legs straightened. Giving me a kiss on the forehead, he grabbed his car keys and phone and admonished me to eat something and rest before running down the hallway, slamming the front door in his wake.

The moment the door closed, I stumbled, then leaned against the cool metal surface of the stainless steel refrigerator door. Slowly, my legs gave out, and I slid down its smooth surface till I was sitting on the floor. I placed my face in my hands and burst into tears.

When I had exhausted myself, I crawled on my hands and knees a few feet till I could reach up for the strap of my purse. Pulling it off the counter onto the floor, I reached for my cellphone. I dialed the first number in my contacts.

"Are you okay?"

I burst into tears again.

"Hold on. I'm coming to get you."

I sniffed. "Grab my passport."

CHAPTER 26

Mikhail

"Where is she?"

After tearing through Gregor's house, I finally found Nadia's partners in crime, Samara and Yelena, in Samara's painting studio.

Samara turned at my outburst, paintbrush held aloft. Yelena didn't even bother to turn away from her task of hanging one of the canvases stacked against the wall.

Yelena called over her shoulder. "Where is who, Mikhail?"

I clenched my fists, reminding myself these were Gregor and Damien's women and Nadia's best friends.

"You know damn well who. She's not at my place and not here. She has nowhere else to go, so where is she?"

Samara put down her paintbrush and snatched up a stained white towel and wiped her hands. "Is that maybe because you burned down her apartment and jewelry shop?"

I ran a hand over my face and let out a deep sigh. I deserved that. "Please, girls. I'm worried about her. We didn't part well — there were things said — and things not said."

I should never have left her. I should have ignored that damn phone call and stayed right where I belonged, between her thighs, kissing her. Regret twisted deep in my gut. I shattered her with my demands and hard truths and then left her to pick up the pieces. I was a fucking monster. I knew better. I knew she was just testing my new boundaries. I should have kept my anger and lust leashed. Now that I had finally allowed myself to claim her as my own, I had this crushing fear that someone or something was going to take her away from me. It led me to pushing her too hard, too fast, too soon — literally.

I took what she was saying at face value because it was what I wanted to hear, but I knew better. I knew better than to believe her when she said she was comfortable with the level of rough sex I enjoyed. She was a goddamn virgin, and I fucked her like a whore — several times. Slaking years of pent-up rage and desire on her tiny body with no regard for how overwhelming all this must have been for her.

And then I had to go and demand she marry me.

It wasn't how I'd intended it to be. It had been my plan to propose over a romantic dinner, with flowers and champagne and everything her little heart probably desired out of a marriage proposal. My sweet girl deserved that. But then she started fighting me and something primal and untamed swelled in my chest, a deep dark fear that she might leave — that she might leave me.

So I'd reacted the only way I knew how, the way they had conditioned me from birth to react — violently. I saw red. My one driving need was to make her understand *no* wasn't an option, that *no* would never be an option where we were concerned. Those days were over. The days of denying how we felt for one another were over. The harder she fought, the more desperately I drove my fangs into her.

Yelena chimed in. "Were the things said, all your plans to railroad her into a life and a relationship she wasn't ready for?"

Samara piled on. "Was one of the things *not* said a romantic marriage proposal?"

Fuck me, this must be hell.

I'm in hell.

I glanced over my shoulder, practically pleading in my mind for Gregor or Damien or both to walk through that door and save me from their women.

Yelena approached me. "What is on your coat?" She brushed at a few stray flower petals that clung to the wool material.

I shifted my gaze. "There was... an incident."

That was putting it mildly. I had returned home with flowers and that professional pearl and bead drilling machine I knew she'd been wanting. The one with the hundred-and-eighty degrees rotating jaw and water holding post. I knew it was her dream to branch into pearls with her jewelry designs. I had overheard her saying so to some asshole at the wedding party. The man was in the presence of the most amazing woman in the world, and he couldn't even bother to pay attention to what she was saying, but I was listening.

All I'd done these last few years was watch and listen from afar, and yet when I finally had her in my arms, I stopped hearing her. When I realized she wasn't home, I took my rage out on the colorful bouquet in my hand. Not one of my finer moments.

Samara crossed her arms over her chest. "You know you don't deserve her?"

I answered without hesitation. "I know that, but I'm the only man who truly sees her."

Yelena snorted.

I raised both arms, palms up. "I get it. I fucked up. I finally had her in my arms, and I pushed her away. You have to understand. There will never — never — be a man on the face of this earth who loves her more deeply and completely than I do." I nodded toward Samara. "Up until your wedding, I would have been content to spend my days torturing myself, protecting her, always on the sidelines, just to be near her. But something snapped inside of me. And it wasn't just those bastards who attacked her. It was watching you and Gregor, and realizing I not only wanted that for me and Nadia, but I was also willing to fight heaven and hell to have it. I love her and I can't imagine my life without her."

There was a long pause.

The tension in the room seemed to lengthen and stretch. I shifted from one foot to the other. Then Samara placed a hand over her heart and exclaimed, "Oh my God!"

Yelena let out a long mewing, "Awwwww."

They both stepped close and group-hugged me.

I threw my head back and groaned.

Yep. This is definitely hell.

"This is why men never bare their souls," I grumbled.

They both stepped back. Then Yelena slapped my upper arm. "Did you bother telling her any of that?"

"Or were you a typical Neanderthal caveman, all grab and no talk?" Samara asked.

I answered under my breath.

Yelena cupped her ear. "What was that? I couldn't hear you?"

I lifted my eyes to the ceiling and prayed for patience. Through clenched teeth, I responded, "I was the typical Neanderthal caveman."

Casting my gaze around, I eyed a closed closet door across the room. "Ladies, can you please tell me where you're hiding Nadia? I really need to talk with her."

They exchanged a look.

Samara wrung her hands. "We can't."

"We promised," Yelena shrugged.

With a frustrated sigh, I marched over to the closet and yanked on the doorknob. It was locked, but I could tell it was one of those simple button locks that could be opened from the inside. "Unlock this."

"She's not in there."

"I'm not going to argue with you, Samara. Unlock the damn door," I demanded before turning and slamming my fist against it. "Nadia, get out here. We need to talk."

Yelena shook her head. "He's totally a Taurus."

"Mikhail, she's not in there," Samara complained.

They were lying. Of course, she was in there. It was the only logical place for her to be. I had already searched most of the house. It made sense she'd be close by with her friends. She probably dashed in there the moment she heard my approach without my noticing. I banged on the door again. "Nadia, I'm giving you till the count of two."

I waited. Staring at the doorknob, willing it to turn.

Nothing.

"One. Two," I called out.

It was a simple plywood door with a wooden frame. It took little effort on my part to rip it off its hinges.

Samara and Yelena exchanged another look and said in unison, "Neanderthal caveman."

The dark interior was empty. I shoved aside some of the stacked canvases just in case, but she wasn't in there. I turned on them, fists clenched. My patience was at an end.

Taking a few steps in their direction, I warned, "You're about to see just what a Neanderthal caveman I can be if you both don't start talking."

Yelena's chin jutted out. "You're wasting your breath. We will not tell you anything."

I inhaled through my nose as I tried and failed to rein in my rising temper. Grasping my forearm, I slowly pushed up the sleeve on the black hoodie I was wearing. Then I pushed up the second one. I watched as Samara's slim throat contracted as she swallowed. Yelena's eyes flicked to the door. Unfortunately for them, I was blocking their exit.

I placed my right fist into my left palm. "I didn't want to do this, but you ladies have left me no choice. Just remember you asked for this." I reached into my pocket and pulled out my phone. I looked directly at Samara. "I'm calling your husband," then shifted my gaze and pointed with my phone to Yelena, "and your fiancé, and I'm telling them what you've done."

"No!" they cried in unison as they swept across the room and each grabbed me by the arm. Yelena tried to wrench the phone from my grasp, but I held it up high over their heads.

They took turns jumping against my chest, trying to reach it.

"What the fuck is going on here?" came Gregor's booming voice.

He snatched Samara back by the waistband of her jeans, turning her around to face him. His brow lowered as he demanded an answer from her.

Damien's gaze was equally thunderous as he stormed across the room and grabbed Yelena around the waist. He pulled her back against his chest. "What the hell do you think you're doing touching another man?"

Yelena objected. "I wasn't *touching* touching him. We were just trying to get his phone."

Gregor placed a bent finger under Samara's chin and lifted her gaze to meet his. His voice was low and controlled, which everyone in the room knew meant he was pissed. "May I ask why you wanted his phone?"

Samara bit her lip and looked at Yelena.

"Don't look at her," commanded Gregor, "answer me, malyshka."

"We didn't want him calling you."

Gregor looked up at me. I answered his unspoken question. "Nadia is missing."

"What?" Damien roared. He turned Yelena around to face him. He wrapped his arm around her waist and placed his hand on her jaw. "What do you know?"

"Nothing," she protested.

"What. Do. You. Know?" he repeated.

Yelena huffed. "I know she's not here."

Damien reached for his belt buckle. "Oh, moy padshiy angel, you know a great deal more than that, and you're going to tell me."

"She ran away," offered Samara in a rush.

My brow furrowed. "What?"

She shrugged. "She ran away from home."

"We called it… Operation…." her voice faded away as Damien took several steps forward, pinning her against the wall.

He placed a hand over her head and leaned down. "Finish your sentence."

Yelena shook her head, her eyes wide. "I don't want to."

He stroked a fingertip down her cheek. "Oh, but I insist."

Yelena coughed nervously. She lowered her gaze and whispered, "Operation… Fly the Coop."

I paced away a few steps as I rubbed my jaw and tried to calm the rage that swelled deep within my chest. I turned back. "Are you telling me you helped her leave? She's out there, God knows where, all alone less than a day after someone tried to fucking kill her?"

Samara stamped her foot, which would have been

much more effective had she not been wearing thin ballet slippers. "It's all of your fault. All three of you. If you hadn't treated her like a piece of property to be bought and sold, this wouldn't have happened."

Gregor gave Samara a hard glare, which I'm sure promised punishing consequences later. "She couldn't have gotten far. We'll check the GPS trackers on the cars and the security cameras. We can also track her phone."

Yelena grimaced. "Her phone is probably turned off by now."

Damien exhaled harshly. "And why would that be?"

Yelena and Samara exchanged a look. Then Samara spoke. "Because she's on a plane to London."

Gregor reached for his phone. "I'll call the hangar and have the plane made ready."

Damien moved toward the door. "I'll go get the car."

"Stop," I called out.

Everyone in the room turned to look at me. "This is between Nadia and me. I'll be the one — the only one — going after her."

Gregor looked as if he was going to object, but then slowly nodded. "Take the plane."

Damien nodded as well, then turned to glare at Yelena. "That is for the best. We're going to have our *hands* full here."

I had a feeling after this stunt, neither Samara nor Yelena was going to be able to sit for a week. Nadia would be in good company. When I got my hands on my babygirl, I was going to tie her to my bed and show her exactly who was in charge. Right after I held her in my arms and told her how much I loved and needed her.

The girls didn't have any other further details other than Nadia was landing at Heathrow. They had deliberately told her not to divulge her plans so no matter how severely they were punished, they couldn't betray her confidence. I had to admire their loyalty to one another. Nadia had shown the same level of loyalty to them when they first ran.

As I turned to go, Samara called out to me, "We're telling you where she is because we know you'll do the right thing. Nadia only thinks she wants this kind of adventure. She needs to learn it's not all it's cracked up to be, but you need to give her the space to learn that for herself. Otherwise, you may never know if she is with you for the right reasons."

Gregor smiled and pulled her close and kissed her forehead, and then growled, "I'm still punishing this cute ass of yours."

Samara blushed and hid her face against his chest.

Gregor held her close and stroked her hair. Looking over the top of her head, he said to me, "Go bring our little sister home."

I shook my head. "I'm going to bring *my kroshka* home."

CHAPTER 27

Mikhail

SHE LOOKED BEAUTIFUL TODAY.

I watched as Nadia exited the Victorian line train at the Warren Street Station. She stopped for a moment before a crimson red mural of an intricate labyrinth maze meant to be a play on the word warren. She then followed the press of the crowd up the escalators.

She was wearing her new pair of Doc Martens. They were the original, iconic 1460 eight-hole black boots with bright red roses stitched into the leather. From outside, I had watched her through the store windows as she clapped with glee after entering their store on Oxford Street yesterday. She'd matched it with a black babydoll dress with long balloon sleeves and a cute, ruffled hem. I had watched her buy the dress a few days ago in Soho at a small boutique on Carnaby Street.

Unfortunately, another man had been watching her as well. I grabbed him by the collar just as he lunged for her. Nadia turned at the commotion and almost spotted us, but by then I had dragged the perpetrator into a small space between two brick buildings. It was a tight fit, probably no more than four feet wide, but I still kicked the shit out of him and left him bloody and bruised in the sludge and runoff from a nearby gutter.

No one was going to ruin my baby's Operation Fly the Coop run away from home trip. If this was what she needed, I was going to give it to her — within reason.

We had both been in London for two weeks now, just not together.

Day after day, I watched over and protected her from a distance. I wasn't worried she'd spot me. I had years of practice observing her closely without her knowledge. I had a tiny spark of guilt over once again stepping on her independence by surveilling her without her knowledge, but only a tiny spark. My need to keep her safe far outweighed any feelings of regret or guilt. I was willing to work through many of her concerns about our future life together, but doing everything in my power to protect her from the known and unknown dangers of the world was not one of them.

With the benefit of a private plane, I had actually managed to beat her to the city. I was there waiting just outside Heathrow as she hailed a black cab. I followed her to the Savoy Hotel. She was not aware of it, but I had already reserved the room directly next to her own. If she was trying to stay off the radar, my baby was truly terrible at it. She had kept her original phone, which made her every movement embarrassingly easy to track. She used her credit card to reserve the hotel room before even arriving. Seriously, the only thing she wasn't doing was posting selfies of herself online.

For the first few days, she did the usual tourist things: a visit to Buckingham Palace, touring the Crown Jewels at the Tower of London, taking a photo of herself with the wax figure of Prince William at Madame Tussauds. It had been easy to blend into the crowd of tourists at each location and still stay within view of her cute figure as she took photos and consulted her guidebook. She came close to catching me at Sherlock Holmes' house. They set the museum up as a traditional Georgian House with narrow stairs, tight corridors, and small rooms cluttered with all manner of decor and objects. I got caught behind a family from Wisconsin and was trapped on the stairs. I was only saved by vaulting over the banister and sneaking behind an employees' only stanchion, a move that got me promptly kicked out.

After that, it was a parade of museums and parks each day. She never talked or engaged with anyone, which left me both relieved and sad. While some people are content to travel alone, I had a feeling Nadia was not one of them. Not everyone enjoyed that level of solitude, especially in a bustling, energetic city like London. Each time she sat alone in a cafe or pub, I would watch as she slowly ate her meal while silently observing the heightened chatter of the tourists and locals about her. Once or twice, I could have sworn I caught her sighing. On more than one occasion, I caught a glimpse of sadness in her eyes.

In those moments, I had to restrain myself from going

to her, but Samara was right. I needed to give Nadia space and time, though every second that passed where she wasn't in my arms was killing me. Apparently, after three years watching her from afar, my patience had truly run out.

It was a good thing she was tiring of her little adventure. The signs were there. Plus, I knew her better than I knew myself. She had stopped going to the tourist attractions. She left her hotel room later and later each morning and had spent long afternoons in different cafes around the city.

Instead of museums, she now walked up and down Hatton Garden, the center of the London diamond and jewelry trade. She would stop at all the black glossy and fresh flower garland shop windows and peek inside: Smith and Green, Berganza, Pasha of London, Webley London. Occasionally, she would go inside and ask to see a few pieces. The shop clerks would pull piece after piece out of the display cases, not understanding her love for the jewelry was the love of a craftswoman, not a buyer.

The one time she did buy, she practically gave me a heart attack. She breezed into Presman Mastermelt, a precious scrap metal trader, and bought a small fortune in platinum and palladium, and then breezed out again onto the dangerous, busy streets of London as if she wasn't carrying close to ten pounds of platinum worth one hundred thousand dollars. I almost had to give up my surveillance right then and there. Thank God she at least took a black cab straight back to the Savoy. I then had to arrange for the General Manager to knock on her door and surreptitiously inform her of the hotel's secure safe that was available for the valuables of all guests.

Today, she strolled past the colorful shops and restaurants on Warren Street to stop in front of a cafe with bright fuchsia painted trim. I waited outside till I could see her order something and find a table in the back. She opened her book, *The Great Pearl Heist*, about the theft of a pearl necklace from a famous London jeweler along Hatton Garden in the early nineteen hundreds, and was soon engrossed. I wondered if she'd gotten to the part where they exchanged the sugar cubes for the pearls. I shook my head. If Gregor and Damien ever found out that I'd purchased the same book Nadia was reading to feel close to her, I would never hear the end of it.

Slipping in with a small group of friends, I faked a limp and sat at a dark corner table. The limp allowed me to order something from a staff member without conspicuously standing at the counter where I might be noticed. Raising the newspaper I had brought with me from the hotel, I observed her from afar.

The cafe she had chosen for today was called Coffee, Cakes & Kisses. She sat alone at one of the tables with a white cup filled with a frothy hot chocolate and garnished with three pink marshmallows on the side. The owners had covered one particular wall in scraps of paper. I watched as Nadia asked for and was handed one of the papers. After digging for a pen in her purse, she wrote something on the paper. A minute or two later she wiped a tear off her cheek. Taking a small push pin, she secured the paper to the wall behind her and rose to leave. I ducked behind my newspaper and waited till she was out the door. Striding over to the wall, I snatched the piece of paper and folded it in half as I left. With an eye on her a few blocks ahead, I opened the paper. It had three questions printed on it in fuchsia ink. Nadia's responses were in black pen.

What is your favorite coffee? *I usually drink mochas, but I like hot chocolate with extra marshmallows if I'm feeling sad.*

What is your favorite cake? *Chocolate with vanilla buttercream frosting.*

What is your favorite kiss? *When Mikhail wraps his arm around my waist and pulls me in close and calls me his kroshka before kissing me.*

I smiled as I folded the paper and placed it in my inside pocket for safekeeping. It was finally time to come out of the shadows.

CHAPTER 28

Nadia

Where the hell was Mikhail?

This was getting ridiculous. I was carrying around my phone. I used my credit card to book the hotel — in my own name. I've been walking around this entire damn city visiting every major tourist location for two weeks now. I've even trudged up and down Hatton Garden countless times, just in case he thought to look for me there, among the jewelry stores. I was doing everything but posting selfies online.

What did a girl have to do to get kidnapped by the man she loves?

Running away from home sucked. I missed Mikhail. Time away had shown me we both had overreacted. Mikhail definitely went into hyper protective alpha caveman mode, but I wasn't exactly innocent either.

There was no doubt I was pushing his buttons and deliberately provoking him. I had no explanation other than testing the boundaries of our new relationship. The truth was, if I hadn't been so sensitive about him and my brothers trying to rule my life and take away my independence, I would have noticed how hard he was trying to make up for burning down my shop and how supportive he was being.

And I would tell him all of this if he ever bothers to show up to drag me back to his cave.

I couldn't really be blamed for wanting what Samara and Yelena had. What could be more romantic or a better affirmation of Mikhail's undying love for me than having him chase me down halfway across the world and drag me home? It was possible he was being all enlightened by giving me space and respecting my wishes. Hoping I would return to him when I was ready, which really should be a good thing. Most women would kill for a man that is sensitive to their needs. Most women, but not me. Call me a bad feminist, but I wanted the caveman. I wanted Mikhail to toss me over his shoulder, smack me on the ass, and announce that I was his and his alone. The problem was, I also wanted him to give me the independence I craved. What a mess. At least there was one thing I was sure of.

No matter what, all choices led back to Mikhail.

He was my first crush, my first love, and I desperately wanted him to be my only love.

With a sigh, I walked up the slick, rain-soaked steps of the St. Martin-in-the-Fields Church just off Trafalgar Square. I was attending their longstanding evening event,

Baroque by Candlelight. Tonight's program would include Haydn and Mozart. I couldn't say they were my favorite composers, truth be told I could take or leave classical music, but it reminded me of home. When other teenagers were blaring rock music in their bedrooms, Damien used to play classical music on his stereo. He was super weird that way.

I entered the hushed interior of the small, ancient church. There had been a church on these grounds since medieval Domesday, hence the name, St. Martin-in-the-Fields. The city of London literally rose around its steeple, where previously there had been nothing but farmland. The six massive chandeliers over the tall, darkly stained pews were lowered and bright with candles. There were also tea light candles set along the upper back of each pew. In front, the cream and gold altar was ablaze with several lit candelabras. The faint scent of frankincense and myrrh from centuries of worship permeated the air. Four musicians dressed all in black sat on spindly wooden chairs set in a semi-circle in front of the altar, tuning their string instruments. I selected a pew in the back off to the right.

As I slipped along the smooth, varnished seat, it was as if the world disappeared. With the tall back of a pew both behind and in front of me, I was in my own private cocoon. Taking off my coat, I put my phone on silent and settled in. I closed my eyes and waited for the opening strains of Haydn's Cello Concerto No. 2, the first composition on tonight's program.

Instead of the light and airy violin opening typical of chamber music from that time period, the dark and somber bass tones of the cello filled the air. I listened for a moment. The music was strangely familiar.

Someone in the pew next to me hummed along. I could tell from the deep baritone it was a man, but because of the height of the pew I couldn't see him. The violins started, and I finally recognized the song. It was the Russian love song, *Dark is the Night*. The song Mikhail sang to comfort me.

The man behind me sang, soft and low, for my ears only.

I have faith in you, in you, my sweetheart.
That faith has shielded me from bullets in this dark night ...
I am glad; I am calm in deadly battle.

I crept onto my knees and peered over the top of the pew. Mikhail sat there looking devastatingly handsome in a charcoal cable-knit sweater and dark jeans.

When he saw me, he grinned and raised his voice to sing. "Znayu, vstretish' s lyubov'yu menya, chto b so mnoy ni sluchilos'." *I know you will meet me with love, no matter what happens.*

With a cry, I climbed over the top of the pew. He caught me in his arms. My thighs straddled his hips as I wrapped my arms around his neck. "You came for me."

He pushed a curl behind my ear, before running his knuckles down my cheek. "Always, kroshka."

I pouted. "It took you long enough. Did you get lost? Have something better to do?"

The pad of this thumb stroked my bottom lip. "Better than chasing my girl across the Atlantic Ocean only to spend two weeks watching her window shop? Nope, nothing comes to mind."

My eyes widened. "You've been here the whole time?"

He wrapped his hand around my neck and pulled me close. Our lips were only a breath apart. I could feel the strong, steady beat of his heart under my right palm as the sandalwood scent of his cologne surrounded me. He really had the perfect boyfriendy scent.

He rasped against my lips. "When are you going to learn, kroshka? From the moment I met you, I've never really left your side. You've been mine to watch over, protect, and love from the beginning."

He claimed my lips in a soul stealing kiss. Damn, could this man kiss. It wasn't just a meeting of the lips. It was all-consuming. His hand on my neck, holding me close. His muscular arm around my waist. The taste of him. The feel of his lips against mine. The way his chest would vibrate with low possessive growls as his tongue swirled around mine, but most especially the hard press of his cock.

I pulled back, but only slightly, breathlessly whispering close to his open lips, "Does this mean you love me?"

He shifted his hips to grind his cock against my inner thigh. "What does that tell you?"

"It tells me you want to f—"

He kissed me again. "Hush, you dirty girl, uttering such profanity in a house of God," he teased with feigned shock.

I shimmied my hips on his lap, pleased when he bit his lower lip, closed his eyes and groaned. "Let's get out of here. It's been two weeks," he pushed his hand beneath the hem of my skirt to caress my pussy through the thin silk of my panties, "and I'm starved."

My cheeks flamed at the naughty implication of his words. "Wait. We're leaving?"

"Yes, I want to get you back to the hotel. Now."

I looked over my shoulder at the softly candlelit altar. Technically, this wasn't a Russian Orthodox Church, but it was still a church. "I thought… well… I thought you were going to…."

Mikhail gave me a bemused smile. "You thought what?"

I sighed. So he wouldn't let me off easy. I deserved it for running away. Tracing one of the cable-knit swirls on his sweater, I rambled, "I thought we were going to get married. I mean you said you wanted to marry as soon as possible and that you loved me, and here we are in a church, and you obviously planned this because that song was not on the program."

He shook his head. "Nope."

"You mean Gregor and Damien and Samara and Yelena aren't hiding somewhere waiting for you to give the signal to start the wedding ceremony?"

"Nope."

"We're not getting married?"

"Nope."

I sat back and met his gaze. "You're not even going to propose?"

"Nope."

My chest tightened at the thought. Had I ruined everything? Had I chased away the only man I'd ever loved with this foolish stunt? Why had I ever let Samara and Yelena convince me this would be a grand adventure that would prove his love for me? "Stop saying nope! Do you not want to marry me anymore?" I braced for his response.

"More than life itself."

"Then… why?"

He shrugged. "I thought it would be fun to date first. You know, do proper girlfriend-boyfriend stuff like going to the movies and out to dinner."

"So we're not getting married today?"

"Not today, kroshka."

"But we will one day?"

He nodded. "When you are ready. Until then, I promise, there will be no more talk of white picket fences and babies."

I shrugged. "Well, there could be *some* talk."

Setting me to his side on the pew, he rose and leaned over the pew in front to grab my jacket and purse. As I stood, he put my jacket on me and zipped it up. It was such a girlfriend-boyfriendy thing to do. He then leaned down to sweep me in his arms. After giving me a hard kiss on the mouth, he said, "Yes, but for now, the last thing I want to do with you is *talk*."

I wrapped my arms around his neck as I rested my head on his shoulder. He really was a Neanderthal caveman, and I wouldn't have it any other way.

EPILOGUE

Nadia

"Oh! It says here that Le Guayaba Verde has a dish called pulpo de Juan Griego. It's octopus served with capers, raisins, and pesto. That sounds different! We should try it. I really want to go here. It looks perfect!"

"Baby," said Mikhail.

"Oh! It says we have to taste something called an arepa. It's made from maize and stuffed with beef and avocado. It's like the national dish of Venezuela, so we *have* to try it."

"Kroshka."

"I also promised Yelena I would pick up a Carolina Herrera signature clutch. Apparently, she is some famous designer from Venezuela who designed for Jacqueline Kennedy."

"Babygirl," said Mikhail as he placed his hand over the

travel book I had been reading different restaurant descriptions from.

I was beyond excited. After a month of begging, cajoling, fighting, and pouting, Mikhail had finally agreed to take me with him on his *business trip* for my brothers.

The last few weeks had been amazing. When we returned from London, Mikhail took me back to his penthouse, and it shocked me to see it completely empty. All the boring beige fake decor and furniture had been removed. He then handed me a printout of all the garage sales in the area for that weekend. We filled it with secondhand furniture, old photos of people we didn't know, and dented tin cookie cans. It was wonderful. We also transformed one bedroom into a workshop for the both of us. Day after day, we sat side by side as I worked on the jewelry I planned to showcase in my new shop with Samara and Yelena, and he cleaned and worked on customizing his guns. I continued to surprise him with my knowledge of weapons, and it turned out I had a knack for customizing them.

We had arrived in Venezuela by a private plane in the very early hours of the morning. We laid low in a small stucco house in a residential neighborhood before making our way into the city at dusk. We were both dressed casually as tourists.

"You know we are supposed to *be* tourists," I grumbled.

"It doesn't mean we actually *are* tourists," Mikhail fired back as he gave one of my ponytails a playful tug.

"Come on. There is nothing to say we can't have dinner afterwards!" I responded with a pout.

I was fast learning that Mikhail was particularly

susceptible to my pouts, especially when I puckered my lips in a small moue. I had never really considered myself a flirt. Truth be told, I was wretchedly awkward at it, but for some reason, it came naturally with Mikhail. I liked watching his eyes darken whenever he looked at my mouth or when I said something deliberately sassy to provoke him into spanking me.

There was just something about how he would growl *my dirty girl* that really did it for me. I really loved how he made me beg for his cock whenever he took my ass. I never would have thought that submitting to Mikhail would actually lead to me feeling more confident and self-assured, but it did. He made me feel beautiful and desired. There was no more hiding behind those dusty shelves in my old vacuum repair shop. With Mikhail by my side, I wanted to experience the world. I had finally come into my own.

My cheeks flushed as I thought of the role-playing he started earlier on the plane.

"Tell me what a bad girl you are," he said against my neck as he scraped his teeth along the delicate skin just below my neck.

"I... I..."

Reaching up, he pinched my left nipple till I cried out.

"Tell me."

"I am a bad girl," I breathed.

"And where do I put my cock to punish my bad girl?"

"Oh God!"

"Tell me, baby. Where am I going to put my cock to punish you for being such a bad girl?" he demanded as he rubbed the top of his thigh against my cunt.

I hesitated, and he pinched my nipple harder. I had no choice but to happily submit.

"In my ass! You're going to put it in my ass!"

"That's right, babygirl. And this time I won't take it slow. Maybe I need to force my enormous fist into your tiny little asshole."

"No! Please, that would… oh God… that would hurt too much."

"Yes, it would. It would certainly be a punishment you wouldn't forget. Wouldn't it, baby?"

"Yes," I whimpered.

He bit my earlobe. "Should I force your little puckered hole to gape with this fist?"

"No!"

He bit my earlobe harder. "Wrong answer. Try again."

With a small sob, I relented. "Yes, whatever you want."

"Remember that from now on. Whatever I want. This little body is mine now. Whenever I want. And my word is now law. You understand?"

He then fucked me till I would have given him my very soul. I would no longer shy away from life. From now on, I wanted danger and adventure. *Roar!*

Even with the setting sun, it was still warm in the Plaza Bolivar. We made our way into the cool of Catedral de Caracas. It was a Romanesque white stone cathedral from the sixteenth century.

Moving slowly so as not to attract attention, we made our way to the nave to the right of the entrance. In the shadows, there was a wooden door secured only with a simple knob lock.

"Bobby pin?"

I pulled the bobby pin from behind my ear. One thick strawberry blonde curl fell forward. Mikhail smiled as he tucked it behind my ear. Giving the tip of my nose a quick kiss, he bent to make quick work of the basic lock.

For such a beautiful church, the stairs leading to the bell tower were ugly and industrial looking. At the landing, the metal staircase abruptly and awkwardly ended and was replaced by a set of wooden stairs which looked like they dated back to the sixteenth century. Mikhail carefully stepped on the narrower step and tested his weight.

"Seems solid, but I'll go first."

He climbed the few stairs and raised his arms over his head to push up the floor trapdoor which led to the top of the tower. After climbing up, he motioned for me to follow. Despite being open on all four sides, the air felt stale and old. Replacing the trapdoor, Mikhail hunched down and looked up into the wide mouth of the massive cast-iron bell. He reached up, and there was a loud tearing sound before he pulled free a package secured to the bell with duct tape. Laying it on the dusty wooden floor, he flipped open his boot knife and cut away the rest of the tape. After unrolling the blanket, a Barrett M82 came into view. It was a decent sniper rifle that was pretty popular with the Army.

"So, this guy is a dirty politician who's been stealing our gun shipments to use the weapons against his own people to keep them oppressed and scared?"

"Yep," Mikhail said as he checked the .50 BMG centerfire cartridges in the ten-round detachable magazine. "It's why he has to die today."

I looked out over the Plaza Bolivar. It was a wide-open square in the center of Caracas. It was popular for large political rallies. On the other side of the plaza, there was a platform with a podium flanked by two massive speakers. They had decorated the staging with festoons in the Venezuelan flag colors of blue, yellow, and red. There had been a great deal of economic hardship which, as it inevitably does, had led to a great deal of upheaval.

The man scheduled to give a speech in about a half an hour was dangerously conservative and very anti-American. The CIA wanted him dead, which meant they would actually owe a favor to my brothers and Mikhail for making it happen. That was probably one of the biggest surprises I learned after I finally started asking questions about my family's business. How often Gregor and Damien agreed to help different governments take out disreputable troublemakers. For a fee of course, off the books.

This type of arrangement also helped sell their product. Apparently, they had several clients interested in a shipment of Barrett M82s they had just acquired. Letting it be known that was the gun that had taken care of a certain Venezuelan politician would up its value and start a bidding war.

On the plane here, I'd asked Mikhail, "How do they hide the money?"

"As far as Congress is concerned, I am a subcontractor under an indefinite delivery indefinite quantity contract who is designing a stronger shoelace for regulation army boots."

"Seriously?"

Mikhail shrugged. "There is over $130 billion a year spent on these types of contracts. I'd say a strong twenty percent of them go to pay black op CIA operations like political assassinations."

Now we were holed up in the bell tower, waiting for the cover of darkness. The plaza was slowly filling with people coming to hear the politician speak. Some carried signs. Others just ambled in groups. Still others looked like tourists curious about the crowd.

I turned back to Mikhail. "Are you shooting through an armored vehicle as the target arrives?"

Mikhail shook his head. "No. I'm going to take him out as he steps up to the podium. One clean shot."

I shook my head. "Are you sure a Lobaev SVL wouldn't have been a better choice? It's a much more accurate long-range sniper rifle. We could have fit it with a crazy cool Nightforce 5.5 22X50 NXS telescopic sight."

"Yes, but then the Venezuela opposition would assume the Russians were behind the hit and that would start a whole different set of issues the U.S. doesn't want, at least not yet. And your brothers have crates of Barretts to sell, not Lobaev SVLs."

"Still, the Barrett is best for shooting through military equipment and armored vehicles. Not a hit between the eyes 1200 meters away!"

Mikhail rose and grabbed me around the waist. Placing his hand behind my head, he pulled me in for a kiss. As usual, he took charge, sweeping his tongue in to play with my own, gently biting my bottom lip before delving in for another taste. By the time he was done, it left me breathless and dizzy.

Stroking his knuckles down my cheek, he said, "I love when you talk guns and ammo with me. It's so fucking sexy."

I blushed in response. These last few months, it had been fun sharing a workspace. Mikhail had shown an interest in my jewelry designs and even helped me with the fashioning and welding of some pieces. In return, he was teaching more about the different guns my family sold.

Mikhail returned to setting up the gun just as my phone rang. A photo of Samara from her wedding popped up on the screen.

"Hello!"

"Hey Nadia, I'm not interrupting, am I?"

"No, Mikhail is just setting up the rifle now."

"Good. I just wanted to make sure you're going to make it back in time for the gallery opening."

"Of course!"

Samara was doing a small showing of her work at an upscale gallery in Georgetown as a way to create buzz for our new boutique, Runaway Gallery & Designs. Yelena had hired models who were going to walk around the art show wearing her fashion designs and my jewelry. It was going to be so much fun.

"Gregor's a wreck. He's really nervous for me. He's threatening to buy and then shut down any publication which says anything negative. I think it's adorable. Damien of course won't stop teasing him for it."

Mikhail gave me the signal that he was ready.

"I have to go."

"How exciting! Your first *business trip*. Tell Mikhail I said hi!"

"I will."

I laid my coat on the ground and then kneeled next to Mikhail. He was looking through the scope. Without turning his head, he said, "Kroshka, can you grab the velocity meter out of my bag and get me the crosswind vectors?"

I pulled free the small hand-held device from his bag and turned it on. Holding up the small fan-like portion, I read out the readings to Mikhail.

"Thanks, baby."

I watched him as he adjusted the scope and made other minor adjustments. For the average shooter, this would be a tough shot. Not for Mikhail. It was one reason why he was the best.

But not the only reason.

"Marry me," I blurted out.

Mikhail turned away from the rifle and stared at me for a moment.

I could feel heat rising up my neck and over my cheeks. "I mean… well… if you want to… I mean… I…." I stammered, shocked by my impulsive proposal. "You said when I was ready."

So much for living dangerously and grabbing life by the horns!

I mean, I knew he wanted to marry me and loved me, and I certainly loved him.

Maybe he had changed his mind?

Oh God, what if he had changed his mind?

Had I just ruined the best thing in my life?

Had I just scared off the man I love after already making him wait three years?

Oh God!

With an amused chuckle, Mikhail leaned over and kissed me.

"Is that a yes?" I asked tentatively.

"No."

What?

My heart fell.

I bit my lip as I turned away, not wanting him to see me cry.

Quickly there was a powerful pair of arms wrapped around my shoulders from behind. Mikhail whispered into my ear, "The guys would never let me live it down if they found out you proposed to me. You're just going to have to be patient and wait for me to ask again."

I raised an eyebrow. "Again?" I said, teasing him for his demand I marry him the last time, which was decidedly not very proposal like.

He kissed my nose. "Just for that, I'm going to make you wait a little longer."

I turned my head to caress my cheek against his. "How much longer?"

"If you're a good girl..." He paused and gave me a wink, knowing I was waiting on pins and needles for him to continue. "...later at Le Guayaba Verde, over a dish of pulpo de Juan Griego with some champagne."

I clapped my hands in excitement.

"But first we have to kill this guy, so double-check

those readings and then let me get back to work," he said in a teasingly firm voice.

Dinner was still a few hours away, but he was worth the wait.

The end.

ABOUT ZOE BLAKE

USA TODAY Bestselling Author in Dark Romance
She delights in writing Dark Romance books filled with overly-possessive Billionaires, Taboo scenes and Unexpected twists. She usually spends her ill-gotten gains on martinis, travel and red lipstick. Since she can barely boil water, she's lucky enough to be married to a sexy Chef.

ALSO BY ZOE BLAKE

RUSSIAN MAFIA SERIES

SWEET CRUELTY

Dimitri & Emma's story

It was an innocent mistake.

She knocked on the wrong door.

Mine.

If I were a better man, I would've just let her go.

But I'm not.

I'm a cruel bastard.

I ruthlessly claimed her virtue for my own.

It should have been enough.

But it wasn't.

I needed more.

Craved it.

She became my obsession.

Her sweetness and purity taunted my dark soul.

The need to possess her nearly drove me mad.

A Russian arms dealer had no business pursuing a naive librarian student.

She didn't belong in my world.

I would bring her only pain.

But it was too late...

She was mine and I was keeping her.

SAVAGE VOW

Gregor & Samara's story

Ivanov Crime Family Trilogy, Book One

I took her innocence as payment.

She was far too young and naïve to be betrothed to a monster like me.

I would bring only pain and darkness into her sheltered world.

That's why she ran.

I should've just let her go...

She never asked to marry into a powerful Russian mafia family.

None of this was her choice.

Unfortunately for her, I don't care.

I own her... and after three years of searching... I've found her.

My runaway bride was about to learn disobedience has consequences... punishing ones.

Having her in my arms and under my control had become an obsession.

Nothing was going to keep me from claiming her before the eyes of God and man.

She's finally mine... and I'm never letting her go.

VICIOUS OATH

Yelena & Damien's story

Ivanov Crime Family Trilogy, Book Two

When I give an order, I expect it to be obeyed.

She's too smart for her own good, and it's going to get her killed.

Against my better judgement, I put her under the protection of my powerful Russian mafia family.

So imagine my anger when the little minx ran.

For three long years I've been on her trail, always one step behind.

Finding and claiming her had become an obsession.

It was getting harder to rein in my driving need to possess her… to own her.

But now the chase is over.

I've found her.

Soon she will be mine.

And I plan to make it official, even if I have to drag her kicking and screaming to the altar.

This time… there will be no escape from me.

BETRAYED HONOR

Mikhail & Nadia's story

Ivanov Crime Family Trilogy, Book Three

Her innocence was going to get her killed.

That was if I didn't get to her first.

She's the protected little sister of the powerful Ivanov Russian mafia family - the very definition of forbidden.

It's always been my job, as their Head of Security, to watch over her but never to touch.

That ends today.

She disobeyed me and put herself in danger.

It was time to take her in hand.

I'm the only one who can save her and I will fight anyone who tries to stop me, including her brothers.

Honor and loyalty be damned.

She's mine now.

DARK OBSESSION SERIES

Free to Read in Kindle Unlimited

WARD

Dark Obsession, Book One

It should have been a fairytale...

A Billionaire Duke sweeps a poor American actress off her feet to a romantic,

isolated English estate.

A grand love affair... except this wasn't love.

It was obsession.

He had it all planned from the beginning, before I even knew he existed. He chose me.

I'm his unwilling captive, forced to play his sadistic game.

He is playing with my mind as well as my body.

Trying to convince me it is 1895, and I'm his obedient ward, subject to his rules and discipline.

Everywhere I look it is the Victorian era.

He says that my memories of a modern life are delusions

which need to be driven from my mind through punishment.

If I don't submit, he will send me back to the asylum.

I know it's not true... any of it... at least I think it's not.

The lines between reality and this nightmare are starting to blur.

If I don't escape now, I will be lost in his world forever.

It should have been a fairytale...

GILDED CAGE

Dark Obsession, Book Two

He's controlling, manipulative, dangerous... and I'm in love with him.

Rich and powerful, Richard is used to getting whatever he wants... and he wants me.

This isn't a romance. It's a dark and twisted obsession.

A game of ever-increasingly depraved acts.

Every time I fight it, he just pulls me deeper into his deception.

The slightest disobedience to his rules brings swift punishment.

My life as I knew it is gone. He now controls everything.

I'm caught in his web, the harder I struggle, the more entangled I become.

I no longer know my own mind.

He owns my body, making me crave his painful touch.

But the worst deception of all? He's made me love him.

If I don't break free soon, there will be no escape for me.

TOXIC

Dark Obsession , Book Three

In every story there is a hero and a villain... I'm both.

I will corrupt her beautiful innocence till her soul is as dark and twisted as my own.

With every caress, every taboo touch, I will captivate and ensnare her.

She's mine and no one is going to take her from me.

No matter how many times my little bird tries to escape, I will always give chase and bring her back to where she belongs, in my arms.

Each time she defies me, the consequences become more deadly.

I may not be the hero she wanted, but I'm the man she needs.

Printed in Great Britain
by Amazon